A Candlelight Ecstasy Romance ®

"I WANT YOU TO KNOW WHAT YOU'LL BE MISSING," HE SNAPPED....

Amy opened her mouth to protest, but the sound was cut off by the swift descent of Rick's mouth on hers. She stiffened momentarily at the unwanted invasion, but as her traitorous body began to respond, her lips welcomed him. Her hands crept up and wound their way around his neck, her fingers found his hair, and she pressed his head closer to her own. Her mouth tingled, and a tremor ran through her body. She arched closer, forgetting everything but the lovely world of sensation that he was bringing to her, that she was bringing to him. . . .

A CANDLELIGHT ECSTASY ROMANCE ®

PORTRAIT OF MY LOVE

Emily Elliott

A CANDLELIGHT ECSTASY ROMANCE ®

Published by
Dell Publishing Co., Inc.
1 Dag Hammarskjold Plaza
New York, New York 10017

Dell ® TM 681510, Dell Publishing Co., Inc.
Candlelight Ecstasy Romance®, 1,203,540, is a registered
trademark of Dell Publishing Co., Inc., New York, New
York.

ISBN: 0-440-16719-1

Printed in the United States of America
First printing—May 1983

To Charles, who taught me just how sensuous a smart girl could be!

To Our Readers:

We have been delighted with your enthusiastic response to Candlelight Ecstasy Romances®, and we thank you for the interest you have shown in this exciting series.

In the upcoming months we will continue to present the distinctive sensuous love stories you have come to expect only from Ecstasy. We look forward to bringing you many more books from your favorite authors and also the very finest work from new authors of contemporary romantic fiction.

As always, we are striving to present the unique, absorbing love stories that you enjoy most—books that are more than ordinary romance.

Your suggestions and comments are always welcome. Please write to us at the address below.

Sincerely,

The Editors
Candlelight Romances
1 Dag Hammarskjold Plaza
New York, New York 10017

CHAPTER ONE

The first time Amy saw him, he was leaning against the wall, smoking a cigarette and surveying her insolently. His sardonic grin unnerved her, and she almost lost the thread of the lecture she was giving. Determinedly ignoring his appraisal, Amy turned back to her class and continued her lecture on the comparative bone structure of the bird wing and the human hand.

The hot May sun beat in the windows, making the classroom uncomfortably warm in spite of the air conditioning. Most of the class looked as bored as Amy felt. Surreptitiously she checked the clock on the wall and noted with relief that the class was almost over and that in just a few minutes the bell would ring, releasing both Amy and her students to freedom for the rest of the afternoon.

Without breaking off her lecture, Amy sneaked a look out into the hall. The stranger was still studying her intently. Amy could not see him too well, but from where she stood he looked tall and muscular, and stood with a kind of powerful grace that spoke of abundant self-confidence and maturity. She wondered if he was waiting for one of the girls in the class. No, she doubted that, although some of the more sophisticated girls probably wished that he were. This man was at least thirty-five and well past any interest in a college sophomore. Then who was he waiting for? Inwardly Amy tried to shrug him off, although it was difficult for her to do so. In any event, it was none of her business. He was not waiting for her.

The bell finally rang, signaling the end of the lecture period. The students gathered their notebooks, and several voices called, "See ya, Dr. Walsh," as they fled out the doors, several of the girls openly displaying interest in the man standing in the hall. Closing her lecture notes and putting them into her satchel, Amy turned off the light and closed the door behind her. She was surprised to find that her mysterious stranger was still leaning against the wall. As she approached him, he straightened and walked toward her. "I'm Rick Patterson," he informed her smoothly. Extending his right hand, he took her small hand in his own and shook it solemnly, although there was a hint of laughter in his eyes, as though he were aware that he was throwing her off-balance.

Amy stared at him blankly, trying desperately to keep the emotion that she was feeling from showing on her face. Was the man trying to pick her up? She knew that she was pretty enough in a prim, bookish way, but hardly the type of woman that had men with this man's dynamic appeal trying to make her acquaintance. Tentatively she withdrew her hand from his and stared up into his startlingly handsome face, gasping inwardly at the sheer magnetism of his dazzling smile. "I'm Amy Walsh," she said quietly, hoping the inner agitation did not show in her voice. "Can I help you?"

"I see that Dr. Thompson hasn't talked to you yet. I understand that you need some difficult photography done for a project of yours. He asked me, as a favor, to contact you about it."

Amy felt yet another emotion clogging her already overloaded circuits, but she willed herself not to be irritated by his referral to her new book as "some project." She reminded herself to be pleasant to this man who, after all, had responded to the request of a friend. "I don't quite understand," she said finally. "Do you know of a photographer who can do underwater work and some shots of microscope slides under thousand power magnification?"

Rick seemed momentarily taken aback, then he smiled dazzlingly at Amy as he took her arm and steered her toward the door. Stunned again by the force of his smile, Amy did not object when he escorted her out of the Life Science Building and across the shady campus. "I'm just as glad that Dr. Thompson has not had a chance to talk to you yet. That way I can make my offer to you myself. Why don't we go somewhere for a Coke and talk?" His deep, warming voice had an unaccountable effect on her, and before she could protest—not that she would have anyway—Rick guided her to the student center.

Amy's mind was whirling. What kind of offer could this man possibly make that would involve her?

The curvaceous young waitress who seated them flashed her violet eyes at Rick, and was rewarded with the same charming smile that he had used on Amy. Amy wondered if every woman Rick came in contact with was similarly rewarded, then chided herself for being cynical. Rick ordered a Coke for her and a beer for himself, and watched with tastefully concealed interest as the shapely waitress swayed across the room. Amy in turn studied Rick through narrowed eyes. Does he have this effect on all women, she wondered, or is it just me? No, he would have definite appeal to almost any female alive. Amy admitted to herself that he was nothing like the men with whom she usually came in contact, and he was much better looking than most of her colleagues. Wavy auburn hair lightly brushed his collar and framed a hard square face with strong even features. Bright blue eyes could study intently or they could dance with mischief, as they were doing right now. Allowing her gaze to travel lower, Amy studied a body that was in superb physical condition under the slightly rumpled jeans and cotton pullover that did not seem to be a uniform of rebellion but Rick's usual work clothes. Amy

11

guessed that when Rick was standing, he was about six feet tall, but his powerful build made him seem even taller. He had wide shoulders that tapered to a narrow waist and flat stomach, but he could not be truly considered slim. The muscles had bulged in his thighs when he walked, and Amy had noted that in spite of his size, Rick had moved with surprising grace. Amy was amazed that his looks appealed to her the way they did. She was usually drawn to a less physical man, and her strong, undeniable attraction to Rick Patterson left her confused. Absently she twisted the tiny rope ring she wore on her right hand, an outward sign of her inward confusion. As some thoughtful soul turned the jukebox down to allow for conversation, Rick turned to Amy and eyed her thoughtfully. "So you need underwater work and some magnification shots," he said finally.

Amy forced herself to quell her interest in Rick's physical attributes and the effect they had on her and get to the topic at hand. "Yes, I need extensive underwater lake shots and thousand power magnification. Will you tell me about the photographer you know of who can do that kind of work?" Unconsciously Amy's voice became authoritative, as though she were in front of a class, and she tapped the table with her forefinger. Rick smiled faintly and Amy winced, realizing how bossy she must have sounded. "Sorry," she muttered. "Teachers do that and don't mean to."

"That's quite all right," Rick replied graciously, although she suspected from the small smile hovering on his lips that he was inwardly amused. "From what you and Dr. Thompson have told me, I'm afraid that Patterson's Pics is probably the only firm in San Antonio that can do that kind of work."

"Oh, dear," Amy said slowly. She had heard of Patterson's Pics, the whimsically named firm that was the top photography studio in San Antonio. The firm's logo appeared in the paper frequently in the fashion pages and in the commercial section. The photography was always first quality. It was also quite expensive.

12

"So you're Patterson's Pics, and you were kind enough to come out here and talk to me about my photographs," Amy said wistfully. "I'm honored and I wish that I could use you, but frankly, short of a miracle, there is no way that I can possibly afford your work."

"I know that," Rick said baldly.

Amy looked at him oddly. "Then why did you come over here?"

"Would you believe that I came out of curiosity? Dr. Thompson said that he had this beautiful young assistant professor who needed some pictures taken, and I thought . . ."

Amy looked at Rick in astonishment, then realized that he was kidding her. She was again thrown off-balance. Other people so seldom made a joke at her expense! Flustered, Amy frantically searched her mind for a clever comeback but came up with nothing. Conceding victory to Rick, she just smiled at him. "No, I wouldn't believe it for a minute," she said lightly. "You said earlier that you had an offer for me. If you were serious, I'd very much like to hear what you have to suggest." Amy's green eyes became businesslike.

"First explain to me in detail exactly what you are doing the pictures of," Rick said smoothly. "Then I will be better able to make suggestions about your work."

"The pictures will be used in my new book," Amy replied, responding instantly to Rick's smooth command. "It's the first major research work I've done since my dissertation. That's the research you do to get your doctorate degree."

"I know what a dissertation is," Rick commented dryly. "I gather that the photographs are an important part of this new book."

"They are crucial," Amy admitted, taking a sip of Coke. "They're so important that I postponed publishing the book until September so I could have them. My book is on the freshwater mussels, or clams, of the Highland Lakes of the Hill Country and the effect of certain parasitic flukes—those are

13

worms—on the mussel population. We are trying to find a poison, or medicine, if you prefer, that will knock out the parasite but not harm the mussels. I've spent the last two years testing various agents and finally I seem to have found one that works quite well. To show the effects of the poison, I need pictures of the mussel beds under the water, microscopic shots of the parasites themselves before, during, and after treatment with the poison, and some photographs of the infested tissue before and after treatment. The pictures will be a major portion of the data in the book." She broke off suddenly, unsure whether or not to continue. She could never tell if she was boring someone with her talk about her pet project.

"Well, as I said, Patterson's Pics is the only company in San Antonio with that kind of expertise," Rick said smoothly. "I assume that you can't afford the work."

"You assume right." Amy laughed. "I have the salary of a rather new faculty member."

"Well, I think I may have a solution," Rick said as he surveyed her speculatively. Solution, or proposition? Amy wondered as he surveyed her thoughtfully, taking in the small high breasts that gently swelled the fabric of her blouse. His eyes traveled lower, gazing through the glass table at her ridiculously small waist and narrow, almost boyish hips, which her snug slacks revealed, then glanced upward at the long slender arms and hands before looking with frank appreciation at her narrow, fine-boned face—sharp but pretty in an old-fashioned way. Amy felt that she was under no illusions about her face or her figure. In the mirror, she saw the kind of shape that other women admired but that men found scrawny, and she felt that her face and figure together lent her an air of firmness and maturity that was not entirely warranted. Underneath Amy's restrained professional manner there lived a fun-loving, romantic, mischievous imp who could get away with murder, simply because no one would ever suspect her of anything. Amy was not totally unaware of the delicate beauty of her slender body and her fine

14

features, but she tended to discount them, since they were not usually appreciated by most men. Yet here was this impossibly attractive man appraising her intimately! The look he gave her was frankly sensual, and Amy caught her breath. Rick smiled faintly at her embarrassment. "I need an assistant for a few hours a day this summer," he said suddenly. "You're off in the afternoons, aren't you?"

Amy expelled the breath she had been holding. What had she been expecting, for heaven's sake? She was hardly the kind of woman that a man like this one would proposition. Exuding masculinity and sensuality, he probably had not had to proposition a woman, any woman, in years. He would hardly be interested in a woman whose allure was of a more subtle nature. Perversely Amy was disappointed at the thought, and disgusted with herself for being so. She forced her mind back to Rick's offer. "Work for you as your assistant?" she asked slowly.

"Is there something wrong with the suggestion?" Rick asked with narrowed eyes.

"Oh, no," Amy said quickly. "But I can assure you that I don't know the first thing about photography."

"That's quite all right," Rick replied in that smooth, deep voice. "I don't know the first thing about mussels, either, but I'm willing to learn."

Although Rick's words had certainly been courteous enough, Amy sensed an unspoken challenge in them. He thought that she felt she was above his job offer! She didn't, of course. It was true that until now her pursuits had been mostly academic, but she had other talents and could easily learn to do whatever was required of a photographer's assistant. However, she was reluctant to accept Rick's offer. Never in her twenty-seven years had she met a man like him. He attracted her and intrigued her, and she was sure that she could not handle him. Despite his teasing manner, she knew that Rick Patterson was a forceful individual and that he was used to getting his own way. Add that to his sensuality, and Rick could be dangerous to her if he wanted to

15

be. And his visual examination and appreciation of her just a moment ago proved that he saw her as a desirable woman. The dry scholars with whom Amy spent most of her time were either unaware of her as a woman or much too polite to indicate that they were, and she simply did not know how to react to this man, who indicated in no uncertain terms that not only did he see her as a woman, but he obviously liked what he saw. Yet she desperately needed the pictures he could take in order to complete her book.

Lifting her chin slightly, she decided to accept his unspoken challenge, whatever the consequences might be later. "If you don't mind training me, then I accept. What would be involved in a job as your assistant?" she asked slowly.

"All kinds of things," Rick replied casually. "I need someone to carry tripods and spare pieces of equipment, answer the phone, set up lights, hold an auxiliary strobe on location shots, do a little nude modeling, write up bills of sale—" Rick looked up and laughed out loud at Amy's horrified expression. "I couldn't resist," he sputtered. "You fell for it so beautifully!"

Amy's face relaxed into a smile as her heart turned over. When he was laughing, Rick's charm was irresistible! She had never met a man with this kind of appeal before! She laughed with him at her own gullibility, forgetting for the moment her vulnerability with him. "Do you really do that kind of thing?" she asked as their laughter subsided.

"Yes, we do, but it would not be expected of you. Still taking the job?" he asked casually.

"Of course," Amy replied with a confidence that she really did not feel. "When do I start?"

"Report the first week of June. You can work four hours in the afternoons during the week and help with the location work on Saturdays and Sundays. Oh, by the way, do I need to make reservations at one of the lodges?"

"No, I stay at Dr. Thompson's cabin, and there is plenty of room." Amy gulped as she volunteered to share the cabin with this incredibly sexy man, but their relationship was strictly business, and it would be ridiculous for Rick to be out the expense of a lodge.

"That sounds fine," Rick replied genially. "Now, pretty lady, I have an appointment across town in just a few minutes. See you in June." With that, he leaned down and kissed her hard on the mouth, then whisked out the door into the bright sunshine.

Amy held her hand to her lips and was astonished to find that her fingers were trembling. My God, she thought, no kiss has ever made me shake like this! The touch of his mouth had been hard and brief, yet the aftertaste tingled on Amy's lips and she was shaking slightly. Never had such a brief caress had the power to reduce her to jelly! Much to her chagrin, Amy forced herself wishing the kiss had gone on longer, and that she had had time to respond to it. And she was going to work for him this summer! What had she got herself into?

Two hours later, Amy was considerably calmer about her decision to work for Rick Patterson. The practical side of her nature had taken over, and she chided herself gently for ever letting her imagination run away with her. Rick's job offer was just a generous favor to his old friend Dr. Thompson, and he had teased her outrageously only because he knew she would fall for it as she had.

Sitting on the sofa in her small cozy apartment, drinking a glass of iced tea, Amy acknowledged that this was probably the only chance she would have to get the pictures that she needed. And if Rick harbored any romantic notions about her, he would drop them as soon as he found out what she was really like. At least Amy assumed that he would. Nearly every other man had. Amy sighed and picked up a pillow. Cradling it in her lap, she thought about all the other men whom she had met over the years and how they had reacted when they got to know the real Amy.

There was nothing wrong with the real Amy. She was not mean or ugly or catty or dull. Far from it. She could be the soul of kindness, she did not harbor a bitchy bone in her body, and she had a ready, if somewhat shy, wit. Amy's big social drawback was that she was brilliant. Not just smart, but absolutely brilliant. Her parents began to wonder about her intellectual potential when, at the age of four, she taught herself to read the back of the cereal box. Subsequent testing when she started school had revealed a rare intellect that her parents and teachers did their best to foster. Consequently, as Amy's mental potential developed, she became known and thought of as a "brain."

Although her abilities delighted her parents and teachers, Amy's young contemporaries were either jealous of her or held her in awe, neither of which made it easy to make friends. As Amy grew older the boys and later the men that she met usually adopted the same attitude, making it very difficult for Amy socially. A man's usual reaction was either resentment of Amy's intellect or an uncomfortable self-consciousness, lest he slip up and say something that would reveal his own lack of brilliance. Perversely Amy refused to hide her intellect behind a Dumb Dora act, and this further isolated her from most men. The tragedy was that Amy was in no way a snob. She enjoyed knowing all kinds of people, and they usually enjoyed knowing her too, until they found out about her above-average intelligence.

As a result of years of unfair treatment, Amy erroneously thought of herself as sexually unattractive. She was supremely self-confident in her teaching and in her research, since she excelled in those areas, but she saw herself the way she thought others saw her—as a brain and nothing more. After one disastrous emotional involvement, which had wounded the sensitive girl deeply, Amy had deliberately shut her mind to the warmth of her body and the sensuality of her nature, since she knew that it was unlikely that one of her fellow academics, the only men who felt remotely comfortable with her, would ever stir her the way a man was supposed to stir a woman.

Amy swirled the icecubes in her empty glass and allowed herself to think about the first man she had ever loved. She had been in graduate school then, a brilliant young student and the youngest candidate that year for a doctoral degree. Miles was a fellow student, but different from most of the other dry scholars. Cute, young, and cocky, he appealed to Amy's adventurous spirit, and she fell for him hard. They were on their way to a good life together, Amy was sure of it.

Then Amy won the prestigious Hathaway fellowship, a generous postdoctoral grant for an additional two years of research, and Miles had been furious. He had been counting on the fellowship himself and refused to believe that Amy was more deserving. Bitter words were exchanged, and Miles left both Amy and the university. Quenching her adventurous spirit and immersing herself in her studies, Amy allowed time to heal the pain left by Miles's defection, but a residue of bitterness remained, which made Amy extremely cautious when she finally started thinking again in terms of a future mate.

Amy had just about given up finding another man when she met David Houston. An assistant professor in biochemistry, he had dated Amy for the past six months and lately had been hinting that he was thinking of asking Amy to share her life with him. He was quite vocal in his desire to marry a bright woman, professed to admire Amy because of her intelligence, and had never exhibited any of the intellectual jealousy that had destroyed her relationship with Miles. Amy sincerely hoped that the relationship between herself and David would work out, because she was basically a loving woman and wanted a husband and children, and she felt that David, with his desire for a wife with a brilliant mind, might be a good chance for her to have that. Yes, she wanted to marry him. But as she prepared a simple supper to share with David, it was not David's kiss that was on her mind.

Leaving a tasty stew on the stove, Amy showered and washed her hair in preparation for her date with David. As she soaped her body she wondered if Rick really found her attractive. Comparing herself to the lush beauties that were a photographer's stock-in-trade, she did not think so. She hurriedly toweled her body and stood naked in front of the mirror, blowing her short brown hair dry. Rick had erroneously assumed that Amy was shy about her body. In fact, she was quite immodest, believing her figure to be unexciting, and would wear the briefest of bikinis without batting an eye. She could probably have posed naked for any other photographer without it bothering her in the least. It was the thought of taking off her clothes for Rick that had made her blush. She basically would not have cared whether any other photographer found her attractive, but she would have cared what Rick thought. Disgusted with herself for the direction that her thoughts were taking, she ran a comb through her expensive haircut and rushed to her bedroom as the doorbell sounded, pulling on her jeans and a top. Breathlessly she opened her door to greet David, who was waiting patiently on the landing.

"What took you?" he teased. "I thought you had forgotten about tonight."

"Sorry," Amy said as she dropped a light kiss on his cheek. "I was getting dressed."

In most other men this would have elicited a leer, a grin, or at least a knowing look. David did not respond except to stroll into the kitchen and lift the lid of the stewpot. He fished a spoon out of a drawer and tasted the stew gingerly. "Needs more salt, hon," he offered gaily.

Amy took the spoon out of his hand and tasted the stew herself. "Tastes fine to me," she said lightly. "You can add more at the table if you want."

"Okay," he replied cheerfully as he ran his fingers through his shock of bright red hair. The hair was a direct contrast to his calm, almost bland personality. "Did you like that cookbook I bought you?"

"I haven't even had a chance to look it over," Amy said, "although it does look interesting." She appreciated David's thoughtfulness in buying her the book, since she had specifically said that she wanted it, but sometimes Amy had the feeling that

David was trying ever so subtly to groom her for her upcoming role as Mrs. David Houston. Although, she had to admit, David tried to please her too, taking her to the corny romantic movies that she loved, to munch on cartons of popcorn while she wallowed in the syrupy stories. They had a lot of different tastes and tried to please each other, but sometimes Amy balked and at other times she could feel David rebelling. They had a lot of things to work out yet.

Amy took the plates and cutlery from the kitchen and set the small dining room table, then tossed a green salad while David made large glasses of iced tea. He brought the salt shaker and the stew from the kitchen and they sat down to supper, spending most of the meal talking about the progress David had made on his own research project, a study of the immune system's response to various toxic chemicals. Amy had been watching his progress closely and was able to discuss his project intelligently, although she was careful not to make any suggestions or give any friendly advice, since several times in the past David had seemed to resent her doing so. It was not until Amy had brought out large bowls of chocolate ice cream that her book was even mentioned, and then David was the one to do so.

"By the way, how's your work coming? Will you be able to get the pictures that you need? I think they will make the difference between a good book and a super one."

"Thanks," Amy said softly. "As a matter of fact, I found someone today. Patterson's Pics is going to do them for me."

"Patterson's is awfully expensive. Is tightfisted Thompson letting go of a little of that precious department money of his?" David asked a bit eagerly. The assistant professors were usually expected to pay their own writing and publishing expenses, but occasionally grant money was made available to some of the faculty members for publication work.

"You just want to weasel a little of the money for yourself," Amy teased, laughing when David turned a fiery shade of red. "No, as a matter of fact, I'm paying for it myself."

21

"Oh, well, no money for me." David sighed. "But if you aren't getting department funds, how are you going to pay for the work?"

"I'm going to work for Patterson's Pics a few hours a day this summer in exchange for the pictures."

David's response was not what Amy expected. "That's nice," he said flatly. He got up from the table and carried the dishes to the sink.

"What's wrong?" Amy demanded as she scrambled up from the table and followed David into the kitchen.

"I thought we were going to spend some time together this summer," David said levelly.

"We are," Amy replied. "I'm only going to work a few hours a day and help with the location work."

"Add that to your teaching schedule and the time you spend researching at the lake and you won't have much time left." David returned to the dining room and picked up their empty glasses. Amy followed with the empty salad bowl. David started washing the dishes vigorously as Amy scraped the almost-empty stewpot into the garbage.

"You'll see lots of me," she protested. "And you know I need those pictures to have the best book possible."

"Look, I know you need the pictures," David said. "I'm just jealous of the time you'll have to spend working for them."

"Thanks," Amy said softly, although she couldn't understand why David was so jealous of her time. It wasn't as though they were the most possessive couple in the world. They loved each other, but the romantic possessiveness that Amy took for granted in the fantasy romances that she loved to read about did not happen in real life. She and David each had their own lives to lead, and surely a few hours spent apart were no big deal. "Maybe if the book is good, they'll consider me for an associate professorship and tenure."

"They might not consider you for that even if the book is good.

But it will be good, Amy, especially if Patterson's does the pictures. You know that."

"I want it to be more than just good!" Amy replied with shining eyes. "I want it to be the best."

"Don't knock yourself out over it, Amy," David said with concern. "Remember, you'll probably be marrying soon and retiring in a few years to have babies," he added as he let the water out of the sink and folded the dishcloth.

"I'll what?" Amy asked absently.

"I said that you'll probably retire in a few years to have babies," David replied. "Little redheaded babies."

Amy looked at David with a growing sense of disbelief. Yes, she wouldn't mind having a baby or two, but did he really think she would retire and limit herself to that? She had a mind that had to grow and be challenged constantly, or she would choke in frustration. She would have to keep working in her field, keep researching, keep learning new things, keep writing, because she could do no less. She did not insist on perfection in her book in order to compete with her fellow professors. She did not need to do that. She insisted on perfection because she was capable of producing it, and she would accept nothing but the best from herself.

As though sensing her withdrawal, David pulled her over to the sofa and sat down beside her. "At any rate, I'm glad you're getting the pictures," he said softly.

They sat in comfortable silence for a few minutes, then David reminded Amy that he had put in a long day and said good night. They shared a brief kiss at the door, and Amy watched him uneasily as he walked down the stairs and out of the building. She had honestly thought that David would be the man for her, the one who would understand her need to learn, to grow, to continue with her promising career. Tonight David revealed feelings and opinions that Amy would have preferred not knowing.

23

Amy curled up in a ball on the sofa and nibbled her fingernail. Involuntarily she thought of Rick Patterson. She wondered briefly as she relived his brief shattering kiss if he would want her to quit her job if they were married.

CHAPTER TWO

The hot June sun bounced off the white stone walls of Patterson's Pics as Amy drove her Nova around to the employee parking lot in the back and eased it into the only available space. Locking her doors, she walked around the building and pushed open the glass front door and walked into the small foyer. A peculiar smell, something like vinegar but sharper, assaulted her nostrils, and she sniffed the air in curiosity. The room held a comfortable sofa and a table piled with old magazines, but was otherwise empty. The walls of the foyer were lined with a variety of commercial-type photographs that looked gorgeous to Amy's inexperienced eye. She guessed that these were samples of the kind of work Patterson's Pics did.

A middle-aged woman opened the door leading to the back and called out to Amy. "Are you the girl who's going to make my life bearable this summer? Don't stand out there all day—come on in and we'll make you at home."

Amy walked over to her and extended her hand. The woman shook it warmly as she looked Amy over. Amy studied her with equal curiosity. The older woman was somewhere in her forties, yet was dressed as youthfully as a teenager in tight jeans and a

Western shirt. Her figure was still slim, but her face showed the passage of what Amy guessed had not always been easy years. Her laughter was genuine and her smile was warm as she noted Amy's equally tight jeans and cool top. When Amy had called to find out when to report for work, an anonymous friendly voice advised her to dress in jeans or the equivalent because, "There's no tellin' what you may have to climb up on over here." Amy now guessed that the voice on the phone had belonged to this woman.

"I see you listened to my advice," she said in confirmation of Amy's thoughts. "I'm Betty Jean Travers, and I'm the secretary-bookkeeper for Patterson's Pics. Rick's out on a job right now, but he told me to show you around and then put you to work. Come on back and I'll give you the tour." Amy instinctively liked the smiling woman who had greeted her so warmly.

As she followed Betty Jean through the swinging doors to the work area, Amy was conscious of a vague feeling of disappointment that Rick had not been present to greet her. She had not seen him in the month since he had commandeered her and offered her a job, but more than once she had thought about him and had relived his hard, brief kiss, and a part of her had looked forward to seeing him again. Inwardly scorning herself for the disappointment she felt at not seeing the attractive man, she hurried after Betty Jean into an open room from which several other doors led to the other parts of the studio. One end of the room housed a large cluttered desk with the usual telephone and typewriter, and on a table behind the desk sat an obviously brand-new computer console and screen. Out in the room, there sat several large work tables, and a waist-high work counter lined three walls of the room. On the counter several different cameras were mounted vertically on metal frames to focus permanently on the white counter top. Betty Jean gestured to the cluttered room. "This is the general workroom and gossip center."

"What are those cameras mounted like that for?" Amy asked.

"Those are used exclusively for copy work," Betty Jean replied. "We can copy slides and photographs as well as shoot small objects and papers on those. Most photographers hate that kind of work, so stay away from them when they're doing copy."

Betty Jean led Amy through the first of the mysterious doors leading from the workroom. They went around a tunnellike bend and came to another door, this one shut tight and sealed around the edges with rubber insulation. Betty Jean knocked sharply on the door and waited a moment for a reply. When none was forthcoming, she opened the door and ushered Amy into what was obviously a darkroom. The smell of vinegar was almost overpowering in there. Various pieces of equipment lined a waist-high cabinet, and Amy recognized an enlarger sitting to one side of a row of trays. "This is the black-and-white darkroom. Old-fashioned as all getout, but Rick insists that for black-and-white, the old way is still the best way." Betty Jean turned around and they left the room. "Never open that door without knocking and waiting for a reply. Usually the photographers lock it behind them, but if they forget, you could ruin several hundred dollars worth of work in a flash."

Amy nodded wordlessly as she followed Betty Jean to the next room. This room housed a square machine that had a spaghetti-like strand of film feeding into one end of it and a strip of color prints coming out of the other. No one tended the machine, but computerlike controls covered a large portion of its top. Betty Jean looked with admiration at the machine. "This is the new color printer. For his color work, Rick insists on the most modern equipment."

"You mean the most expensive and the most troublesome damned machine that he could find," a strangely musical voice growled in Amy's ear. Amy jumped, but Betty Jean turned around and cheerfully punched the owner of the musical voice in the arm.

"Just because you aren't smart enough to run it without hollering for help, don't run down the poor hunk of metal!" Betty

27

Jean laughed. "Amy, this is Joe Valdez, senior photographer and chief griper. Joe, this is Amy Walsh. She'll be helping us this summer in exchange for some photography she needs." Mercifully Betty Jean did not go into detail about Amy's profession or her book. Amy would prefer to get to know these people a little better before they knew too much about her.

Joe took her hand into his and smiled charmingly. About her age, he typified the handsome, macho Mexican, down to the expensive preppie clothing, carefully sculptured haircut, and neat handlebar mustache. Obviously this fellow was a success with women, but Amy discovered that he did not appeal to her nearly as much as his boss did.

Taking her by the elbow, he led her from the color printing room back out through the workroom and into a barnlike studio at the back of the building. In there the ceiling was two stories high and the walls were painted a light gray. A stack of furniture and props were crowded into one corner of the room, and on another wall a portable kitchen facade had been partially disassembled to take up less space. In the center of the room a white backdrop framed a display of women's shoes, scattered artlessly in a huge pile of sand that had been raked to look as though it had been blown in the desert wind.

A young blond man, stripped to the waist and sweating profusely under the hot lights trained on the shoes, was shooting pictures of the scene just as quickly as he could. He snapped maybe two dozen pictures at various angles, then screwed a larger, more unwieldy camera on to a tripod and shot maybe a dozen more pictures of the same scene. Finally satisfied, the young man turned off the lights with a sigh of relief and pulled on a Western shirt. Mopping his damp forehead with a towel, he motioned for Joe and Amy to come with him through yet another door into what turned out to be a real kitchen. He pulled three Cokes out of the refrigerator and handed one each to Amy and Joe. He took a long drink out of his Coke and turned to her. With a start, Amy realized that he was probably not out of his teens yet. Taking a drink of her own Coke, she smiled warmly at him.

"I'm Tommy Lee Andrews, ma'am. Delighted to make your acquaintance."

At first Amy thought that Tommy Lee was a drugstore cowboy, but as they chatted amiably for a little while, she decided that he must really be a country boy. He was too genuine to be anything but an authentic product. She promised herself that as she got to know him, she would find out how a country boy had become interested in taking pictures for a living.

Betty Jean stuck her head in the doorway and reminded Tommy Lee that he had a shooting assignment in just a few minutes. Tommy leaped up, grabbed camera cases out of a closet in the workroom, and practically ran out the door. Betty Jean laughed as the door banged shut behind Tommy Lee. "Rick is really great to work for, but there's hell to pay if anybody is late for an assignment," she admitted. "He has an obsession about punctuality."

Amy made a mental note to abandon for the summer her usual habit of being ten minutes late for everything.

"I guess that's the grand tour," Betty Jean said. "Come on over here and I'll put you to work." She sat Amy down at a small table behind the main desk and handed her a record book and a pad of bills. "I'd like you to write out some of these bills for me and address them to the proud owners. This damned computer is supposed to do it for us, but I can't figure out how to work the fool thing, and Rick hasn't had time to do it himself." Amy promised herself that she would sit down with the computer manual some afternoon and see if she could get the system to work.

As Amy addressed the bills she realized for the first time just how expensive Patterson's Pics actually was. She had known that they were expensive, but she had had no idea of the princely fees charged by the company. She could not pay back the value of her photographs if she worked for a solid year! Of course, Rick was letting her work mostly as a favor to Dr. Thompson, but she still would be in Rick's debt, and that thought made her uncomfortable.

Working steadily, Amy did not hear the door open or see anyone approach the desk until a shadow fell across her work. Amy looked up, expecting to see Rick, and was disappointed when she encountered not laughing blue eyes, but shimmering brown ones. Apparently Joe had sized her up and decided that she was worth his attention. Swinging his booted foot, he was perched on the side of the desk and smiled at Amy charmingly, stretching out his hand seductively and brushing a strand of hair off Amy's brow.

"What's your sign?" he said in a practiced purr.

He had to be kidding! But one look at his dark eyes told her Joe was quite serious. When was the last time she'd been delivered such an obvious line? She couldn't remember. But Amy decided to play along for a few minutes. Flirting with an attractive man was fun and good for the ego, and Amy was as willing as the next woman to flirt a little. "My sign?" she asked innocently. "High voltage."

Joe looked at her in astonishment, then laughed out loud. Smiling ruefully, he picked up his camera case and wandered away.

"How high a voltage?" a familiar, teasing voice whispered in her ear.

Whirling around to confront Rick, Amy realized that he had overheard her dismiss Joe and she colored in embarrassment. "I thought I would have to rescue you from the office Lothario, but it seems that you didn't need any help!" he said as he laughed at her discomfort.

"He's all right as a friend, but that's the only way I want him," Amy said wryly as she leaned back in her chair and looked up into Rick's face. If anything, she had forgotton how handsome Rick was in the month since she had seen him. His vitality seemed to fill the small work space, and Amy swallowed nervously in response to the powerful pull she felt toward this man. She could not tell whether the attraction she felt was sensual or emotional, but it was very real, and Amy realized that it put her in a rather vulnerable position with Rick.

Grabbing her hand, Rick pulled her up out of her chair and said, "Leave that and come in here," as he strode into the barn-like studio. "I have a Zippy's fried fish ad to shoot in less than an hour and I need some help."

"I don't know the first thing about this," Amy said nervously as she twisted the little ring on her finger.

"Just do what I tell you to and you'll be fine," Rick said as he disappeared into the kitchen. "Get out a frying pan and some grease," he ordered as he took a package of raw breaded fish sticks from the refrigerator.

Amy opened the cabinet beside the stove and found a frying pan and an unopened can of shortening. She hunted around in the drawer until she found a can opener and a large spoon. She opened the shortening and gouged out several large spoonfuls to put in the frying pan. Rick took the pan out of her hand and set it on the stove. He adjusted the heat to a low setting, and when the grease had melted, he unwrapped the package of fish and unceremoniously dumped the breaded sticks into the barely bubbling grease. When the fish had turned an attractive shade of golden brown, Rick flipped them over with a spatula. When the bottom side had turned the same shade, Rick carefully removed the half-cooked fish to a draining platter. Amy had watched Rick silently as he worked, but now she felt compelled to speak. "That fish is only half done," she pointed out.

"Brilliant deduction," Rick mocked as he walked into the studio with Amy at his heels. "But we're going to photograph that fish, not eat it. Properly fried fish is brown, which doesn't look right in a picture."

"So you only partially cook the fish so it gets that luscious golden look," Amy concluded.

"That's right," Rick said as he dragged a section of the disassembled kitchen cabinet out into the middle of the room. "Why the hell can't Tommy Lee ever take down his stuff?" he muttered as he maneuvered the cabinet around the shoe display.

"He was late for an assignment—" Amy began, then clamped her mouth shut when she realized that she might get Tommy Lee into trouble. "Do you want me to move the shoes?"

"Yes, and sweep up that sand," Rick said. He disappeared into the workroom as Amy began piling shoes back into the shoe boxes stacked against the wall.

Rick returned with a folding table and several large lights on tripods and began arranging them around the table. Amy put the last of the shoes away and stacked the boxes back against the wall. Rummaging in the kitchen, she found a broom and a dustpan and swept the sand into a pile. Rick found a red-checkered tablecloth and carefully arranged it over the table. He unplugged several of the large lights Tommy Lee had used to shoot the shoes and arranged them around the cabinet.

Amy carefully swept as much of the sand as she could into the dustpan. "Where shall I dump this?" she asked.

"Save it," Rick ordered as he pointed to a heavy plastic sack. "We use it pretty often."

Amy scooped up the sand while Rick carefully hung a large white backdrop behind the table. Going into the kitchen, Rick unwrapped a Zippy's platter and motioned Amy to join him. "Arrange these fish sticks to look as visually appealing as you can, and don't break any if you can help it. They only sent me one sack of fish, the cheapskates."

"Who is 'they'?" asked Amy as she carefully transferred the fish sticks to the platter. "Did Zippy's hire you for this?"

"Not this time," Rick replied as he filled two Zippy's paper cups with Coke. "Zippy's uses a local advertising agency and the agency in turn hires me. The companies that do their own advertising hire us directly."

"Does your company do only advertising photography?" Amy asked as she handed the platter to Rick.

"We do any kind of commercial or event photography," Rick said as he arranged the fish platter and Cokes on the portable cabinet. "Advertising, legal work, conventions, Chamber of Commerce stuff, weddings, private work, such as I'm doing for you—everything except portraits."

"Why no portraits?"

"People aren't willing to pay our prices for portraiture, and trying to get Grandma looking like she did years ago and baby darling to quit bawling and smile for the nice man is not my idea of fun," Rick said bluntly.

Well, that's reason enough, thought Amy. Aloud she said, "Then why do you shoot weddings? It seems to me that wouldn't be much better than portraiture."

"Money," Rick said succinctly. "Besides, I like wedding cake." His face split into its familiar devilish grin.

Amy smiled back. Rick in this charming mood was irresistible, and she again felt a surge of attraction for him. Looking at him now, dressed as she had seen him last, in jeans and a pullover top, she thought how much more attractive he was in his perpetually rumpled state than the slickly groomed Joe or conservatively dressed David. His wavy hair was slightly mussed, as though he had run his fingers through it, and Amy fought an urge to reach up and curl her own fingers into the auburn waves. Get hold of yourself! she admonished herself fiercely. He is just your employer. Why, he would have a good laugh if he knew that the little bookworm was attracted to him.

Rick's voice broke into her thoughts. "I want to show you how to set up lights, so that you'll be able to do it for us when we need you to," he was saying. Amy jerked herself out of her reverie and nodded her head. "The object of lighting these setups so brightly is to eliminate any shadows on the object being photographed," he explained. "If the camera catches a shadow, it will show up in the final picture. We can correct it in the darkroom if we have to, but it's easier to take care of it out here." He stepped back from the lights. "We have a few minutes. You try adjusting the angle of the lights so that the platter and Coke-filled cups are completely clear of shadow."

Amy reached up and started to move one light. "Ouch!" she exclaimed. "Why didn't you tell me it was hot?"

Rick looked faintly amused. "I thought you would know, being a science professor and all," he mocked.

"Very funny," she muttered. Careful to touch only the tripods, she moved first one light and then the other, trying to eliminate the annoying shadows that popped up first in one spot on the platter and then another. After several exasperating minutes, she reached out and moved the platter of fish. That didn't work. Instead of the shadows going away, they became larger and the platter was now off-center on the cabinet. Amy returned the platter to its original spot, then again tried to adjust the lights, burning her hand again. Silently Rick handed her an asbestos glove. Amy tilted the lights slowly, rejoicing as the shadows shrank and groaning as they became larger. Finally only one small shadow remained. Rick put his hand on her arm and stood close behind Amy as he guided her movements. She could feel the warmth of his body through her thin blouse, and her own body clamored in response. Amy forced herself to ignore Rick's closeness and concentrate on moving the last light into place. Slowly the last shadow shrank and disappeared. Amy sighed in relief. "That's harder than it looks," she said.

"You did quite well," Rick commented. "It is hard." He did not move away from her, and Amy swallowed nervously. She was trapped between his body and the lights, and if she backed away, she would bump into a tripod and ruin the lighting. Rick inched even closer to her, and Amy's heart pounded in her throat. He bent his head and sought her lips with his own, finding hers with startling speed and accuracy. Standing frozen between Rick and the hot lights, Amy clenched her hands at her sides, willing herself not to respond, then as the warmth of Rick's mouth penetrated her consciousness, she allowed her hands to creep up and tangle in the curling auburn hair that brushed his collar. Rick sought nothing further, just teasing and tantalizing Amy's mouth until she ached for more. As Rick drew away, Amy felt herself melting into him, and when Rick took her arms to stop her progress, she backed away in hot embarrassment, knocking into one of the lights and sending it crashing onto the floor. "Oh, damn," she snapped to mask her mortification. "I'll have to redo those lights and they're hot."

"That's not all that's hot in here," Rick jibed mockingly as he righted the hot light.

"Excuse me," a very young voice said at the door.

Rick motioned the little teenager into the room and introduced her to Amy. "Stella will be our model today," he said as the girl scurried off to the dressing room.

Betty Jean appeared in the doorway. "Telephone, Rick," she called. Rick left the studio and picked up the extension in his office. Taking a deep breath to regain her composure, Amy wandered over to the desk, mainly to get away from the hot lights, but also in order to get a glimpse of Rick's private domain. The door to his office had been shut earlier but now was standing ajar, and Amy gave in to an irresistible urge to peek inside. She had a theory that she could tell a lot about a person from the kind of office that they had, and Amy wanted to see if Rick's office revealed any interesting tidbits about him. She knew that she was snooping, but she loved doing it, thoroughly enjoying the deliciously guilty feeling it gave her.

Rick's desk was littered with piles of papers and photographs, and the walls were covered with the type of pictures that she had seen in the foyer. A comfortable chair and ottoman were tucked into one corner, and Amy guessed that Rick used that chair as often as he did the one at his desk. On one corner of the desk there sat the framed portrait of a stunning brunette. Dr. Thompson had volunteered the information that Rick was single, so maybe this was Rick's girl friend. As Amy peered in for another quick look, Rick, who had been standing silently, listening, suddenly began to speak.

"Of course, Linda, I wouldn't miss the christening of your new waterbed for anything." He laughed. He lowered his voice seductively. "And I'll even bring champagne. What time will you be looking for me? About nine? Love you, girl."

Amy stepped back, flustered. Well, she had certainly learned something about Rick! She should have known that a virile, exciting man like him would have a lover. Her face became hot as she thought of her passionate response to him in the studio, then she became angry. If he already was involved with a woman, he had no business kissing her like that. She brushed her hand across her mouth angrily and backed away from the office door quickly, before Rick realized that she had overheard his conversation. She ignored her sneaking disappointment. It was none of her business if Rick already had a woman. None at all.

Rick came back into the studio with a camera and a tripod. "Snoop!" he said as he winked at Amy and grinned as she blushed furiously at being caught in her crime.

Quickly screwing the camera on to the top of the tripod, Rick positioned the camera in front of the cabinet and rapidly took a dozen shots of the display. Switching to a small hand-held camera, he used up two rolls of film shooting the display from various angles. He then ordered Amy to turn off the lights around the cabinet and move them. Puzzled, Amy started to question him, but he had moved the platter and the Cokes to the table and was absorbed in adjusting the other set of lights. Amy donned the asbestos glove and unplugged and carried the lights to an empty corner of the room, then watched as Rick photographed the display on the table. He then repeated his command to move the lights. "But aren't you going to need them for Stella?" Amy asked finally.

"Good Lord, no," Rick replied. "The heat from those lights would cook her. I'll shoot her with strobes."

Amy removed the second set of lights. Stella had returned to the studio, dressed in the overalls and kerchief worn by all Zippy's employees, and Rick motioned her over to the cabinet.

He located two strobes in the workroom and brought them into the studio, snapping one on to yet another camera and handing the other to Amy. "Get yourself a stool and put it right there," he ordered, pointing to a spot on the floor that was a little to one side of the cabinet. As Amy scurried to find a stool Rick positioned Stella behind the counter and explained what he wanted from her that day.

When Amy had properly positioned her stool Rick broke off his instructions to Stella and turned to Amy. "Get up on the stool and aim the strobe straight at Stella's face. As Stella moves, the strobe moves with her. Got that?" Amy nodded nervously.

Rick shot two pictures, then reached up and moved Amy's strobe a fraction. He took one more shot, then satisfied, turned to Stella. "Now, Stella, I want your best fresh smile on this. You love Zippy's fish." Amy smothered a giggle, but Rick and Stella were both perfectly serious. Rick kept up a running monologue with her, and she responded to his instructions smoothly.

As Amy watched Rick and Stella she was impressed by the professional rapport between them. Rick shot picture after picture, focusing the camera between shots with lightning speed. He shot several rolls of film, getting some shots of the model holding the platter, some of her just gesturing to it as she smiled invitingly, and an entire roll of Stella tasting a fish stick with a look of gastronomic delight on her face. Amy had to marvel at that one. Rick had not substituted a cooked fish stick but instead had instructed the girl to take one from the platter.

The session with the model lasted almost an hour. Amy's arm ached horribly from holding the strobe in position, and the girl's nose was beginning to shine. Only Rick seemed unaffected by the workout. With a cheerful "That's it, girls," he unloaded the last roll of film from the camera as Amy and the model collapsed. The half-cooked fish was beginning to emit a disagreeable odor, but neither girl made the effort to move the platter. Amy shut her eyes briefly, then opened them to find Stella gone and another woman in the studio. Amy's eyes widened at the sight. She was the one in the picture in Rick's office.

Amy stared in consternation at the beautiful woman, conscious as she was of her own smelly state of dishevelment. The woman standing so confidently in the hot studio was a model of sophisticated chic. Shoulder-length curly black hair framed a strong, classically beautiful face that was enhanced by expensive, expertly applied cosmetics. The woman's tall, Junoesque body and expensive suit were well above Amy's price range, and Rick's arm was around her shoulders in comfortable familiarity. She smiled up at Rick warmly, although she did not return his embrace. They spoke together quietly for a few minutes while Amy's mind whirled. Who was this gorgeous creature? The wife of a friend? A relative? A business associate? A model?

Rick turned the woman toward Amy and drew Amy up off the stool with his free arm. "Samantha, I'd like for you to meet Amy Walsh. She's the one I told you about the other night."

Amy extended her hand to Samantha and was surprised to have it gripped and shaken firmly. "I'm Samantha Westermann," she said in an attractive voice. "Your book sounds fascinating."

"Thank you," Amy stammered. She did not expect Samantha to be so friendly. Up close, Samantha was at least forty, maybe even older, but the maturity of her face and figure only added to her attractiveness. Something familiar about Samantha's name eluded Amy momentarily, then she realized where she had heard the name before. Aloud she said, "I think your boutique is marvelous. I buy many of my nicer dresses there."

Samantha was obviously flattered by that. She smiled and ran her fingers through her thick black hair. "Doesn't Amy remind you of that young woman we met in Mexico?" Samantha said to Rick.

"Yes, now that you mention it, she does look a lot like Toni," Rick replied, as he took Amy's chin in his hand and tilted her face to one side. "But Amy's prettier."

"Yes, you are prettier than she was," Samantha said to Amy. "God, did we have fun on that trip!"

Rick smiled wickedly. "Remember the night we danced until four and watched the sun come up?"

"Do you remember that fabulous meal that we got in Mexico City from that street vendor? That had to be the best fish I have ever eaten!"

"I remember the night we spent in Guadalajara," Rick said softly. "That had to be the most beautiful city in the world."

I don't believe what I'm hearing, Amy thought as Betty Jean burst through the door with a yellow piece of paper in her hand. "Rick, there's a last-minute assignment out at the airport if you want it. Some rich oilman wants pictures of his new jet."

"Is he going to name it, too?" Rick quipped as he took the sheet from Betty Jean.

"I think Lear is such a hackneyed name for a jet," Amy said dryly.

Rick read the assignment sheet quickly, then pulled away from Samantha and headed for the workroom. "I have to do this one myself," he explained as he quickly packed a camera bag and some film. "They want to leave in less than an hour." Planting a quick kiss on Samantha's lips, he hoisted the heavy camera case onto his shoulder and loped out the door.

Amy and Samantha watched him go, then Amy turned back to Samantha and shook her head. "It never stops around here," Amy said in wonder.

"As long as I've known Rick, and that's been a long time, he's always been running out of the door with a camera bag on his shoulder," Samantha said. "But he's a wonderful man, and I love him dearly. Well, I better get back to the shop," she added. "Amy, it was a real pleasure meeting you, and I hope I'll see you again very soon."

I wonder how Samantha would feel if she knew Rick was two-timing her, Amy asked herself as she watched the elegant woman leave the studio. Amy felt a bitter disappointment in the photographer who, in spite of herself, she was so attracted to. What kind of man would cheat on a lovely woman like Samantha? And what business did she, Amy, have being attracted to a man with two women on the string? Amy shook her head as she dumped the smelly fish into the trash. She would have to avoid any more physical contact with Rick in the future. Heaven help her if she fell for a man like that! Yes, she would stick to a man like David. He might not be the most exciting man in the world, but at least she knew where she stood with him.

CHAPTER THREE

Amy released the last curl and carefully laid down the hot curling iron. She pulled a brush through her short hair and fluffed it with her fingers, then yanked open the drawer and withdrew her new cosmetics. Carefully Amy made up her eyes, lining them as the model at Patterson's had shown her in a deep green, and shadowing them in a lighter shade of the same color, and was startled to see her eyes become shadowed and mysterious. She carefully applied mascara to her lashes and a silvery accent to the bone above her eyes and looked a moment at the sensuous green pools that stared back at her. Turning her attention to the rest of her face, she applied just the right amount of blusher and a shimmering raisin-colored lip gloss and smiled at the beautiful new woman who was emerging in the mirror. She grinned a little. She was delighted with the change a little makeup could make, and David was bound to be impressed. In fact, he couldn't help but be. Since her clear skin needed no foundation, she dusted her nose with a translucent powder and declared her glamorous new face ready to party all night.

As Amy slipped on her new jungle print dress she thought about how quickly she had become accustomed to working at

Patterson's Pics and how much, if she were honest with herself, she enjoyed the work. She had seen no more of Samantha since her first day at Patterson's, but she had met a variety of other interesting people since Rick had employed her. The models that Rick hired were an interesting variety of students, housewives, and working women, but they were unfailingly nice and they were very friendly to Amy. In fact, one model had stayed late when Amy expressed an interest in learning to apply makeup more skillfully and had shown Amy how to make the most of her small features. Amy thought again that David was bound to notice the results of that lesson tonight.

In addition to the models, Amy had met businessmen, advertising executives, and several mothers of the bride. The other employees of Patterson's accepted Amy completely as one of them, still not realizing that she was a brain, or perhaps realizing it and not particularly caring. Amy didn't care which was the case, and she enjoyed the camaraderie shared by everyone in the group, including Rick. Although very much the boss, he did not stand on ceremony. As he had on the first day, he pitched in and worked alongside the others.

All week Amy had caught herself watching Rick surreptitiously. After meeting Samantha and hearing Rick's conversation with Linda, Amy had been more than a little disillusioned about him. Of course a man like him would have women. He was much too virile to lead a celibate life, and Amy herself had already found out how easy it was to respond to that sexual appeal that he radiated. But to sleep with two women at once, and not try to hide either liaison? I'm not a prude, Amy told herself over and over, but I just can't go that one. So what did that make her? She was as attracted to him as Linda and Samantha were, and had responded as passionately as she ever had with anyone when he had only given her a simple kiss. How could she condemn him, or either one of the other women, when she was definitely not immune to his charm?

Taking a final look in the mirror, Amy was more than satisfied with the young woman who looked back at her. The short fluffy hair bounced when she moved, and the new dress swirled sensuously around her hips and legs. Amy slipped into strappy sandals and sprayed herself liberally with perfume. David picked her up promptly at eight, and for once Amy was ready on time.

Tonight was a special occasion for both Amy and David. They were attending a cocktail buffet hosted by Dr. and Mrs. Thompson, honoring all of the university's doctoral candidates in biology. This was Amy's first visit to her chairman's home in the two years she had worked for him and her first chance to meet Mrs. Thompson, the woman Dr. Thompson referred to as the love of his life. Amy wanted to know what kind of woman could inspire that kind of devotion. She knew that Mrs. Thompson was an author and a scholar in her own right, and that her intellectual achievements in the field of history rivaled Dr. Thompson's in the field of biology. Amy fervently hoped that someday David would think of her as the love of his life.

To Amy's disappointment, David did not appear to notice the new dress or the glamorous makeup. He grabbed her hand at the door, and with uncharacteristic excitement he said, "Hurry so we won't miss the toasts," and rushed Amy to his waiting Toyota. Amy, tottering on unfamiliar high heels, struggled to keep up with him and collapsed gratefully in the front seat when they finally reached the car. David kept up a steady monologue about the problems he had encountered during the week on his dissertation, but for once it washed over Amy unheard, and he had to repeat a question twice, receiving only a shrug from her in reply. Accustomed to her undivided attention when expounding on his favorite topic, David gave her a puzzled look and drove the rest of the way in silence while Amy savored the soft night air and deliciously anticipated the party.

The Thompsons lived in a rambling brick home in one of San Antonio's elegant old neighborhoods. Pink brick glistened in the moonlight, and ivy covered much of the outside walls of the first story. Inside, the living room was elegantly shabby, and striking impressionistic oil paintings graced the mantel and lined the walls. Eager undergraduates drafted into serving snacks and drinks brought glasses of champagne to Amy and David at the door, and Dr. Thompson appeared magically at Amy's elbow and enveloped her in a warm embrace.

If Amy's efforts to look special were lost on David, Dr. Thompson's reaction more than made up for David's lack of response. "Why, Amy, you look absolutely divine. You're becoming quite sophisticated these days."

Amy laughed as she unconsciously straightened her shoulders. "You wouldn't be referring to the ragamuffin style I usually effect, would you?" she teased.

"He means you don't look like an old maid schoolteacher tonight," a familiar voice said softly at her elbow. "But you do look absolutely beautiful," Rick added, his voice a seductive caress.

"That's all right, Rick." Amy smiled sweetly. "I dress for success. And you don't smell like vinegar tonight, either." She returned his wicked grin with one of her own.

"Touché, Amy." Dr. Thompson laughed comfortably. "I've smelled it on him more than once. Now, if you will excuse us, Rick, neither David nor Amy has met Edna yet." Not giving Amy time to introduce David and Rick, Dr. Thompson took Amy's elbow and guided her across the living room.

What on earth was Rick doing at Dr. Thompson's party? Amy wondered. She knew that Rick and Dr. Thompson were good friends, but Amy could not imagine Rick having the slightest interest in a party made up primarily of academic types. Yet he was not only here, but behaving as though he came to this sort of thing every day. Dressed more formally than Amy had ever seen him, he looked at ease and even more handsome than usual in a fashionably cut three-piece suit in a simple gray stripe and a matching gray shirt and tie. Amy admired the transformation into the successful businessman that a simple change of clothes had achieved, and she was not surprised that the usually rum-

44

pled Rick was equally devastating in more formal wear. Unconsciously Amy compared Rick's appearance to that of David, who was dressed in a not-too-new blue suit and obviously uncomfortable in it. Of the two men, there was no question which one Amy found more attractive tonight.

Inwardly reprimanding herself for making the comparison, Amy followed Dr. Thompson's lead into the dining room and walked with him up to a tall, austere woman with a stern face and iron-gray hair pulled tightly back into a bun at her nape. Dr. Thompson drew Amy forward and smiled proudly. "Edna, this is Amy, the young woman I've told you so much about. Amy, this is my wife, Edna Thompson."

Mrs. Thompson shook hands with Amy as she surveyed the young woman impassively. "Harold has told me so much about you," she said in a curious monotone. She shook David's hand as Dr. Thompson made the introduction, then briefly asked both Amy and David several knowledgeable questions about their research projects. Upon receiving satisfactory answers from both of them, she excused herself and walked through a swinging door into what Amy guessed was the kitchen. Dr. Thompson made no attempt to follow his wife and stood talking with David for a few minutes before moving away in the opposite direction.

Amy stared in stupefaction at the swinging door. Was this the woman that Dr. Thompson called the love of his life? Edna Thompson projected no warmth, no affection, no familiarity toward Dr. Thompson, nor did he, who had always seemed so warm and loving to Amy, show any intimacy toward her. It was as though they were friends and nothing more. Amy had looked forward to meeting Edna Thompson in part so that she could see for herself the kind of relationship that perhaps she and David could hope to share sometime in the future. Amy was somewhat disappointed. Was friendship all she and David could expect to share? Was that all brilliant people ever shared together? Would she, Amy, be as stern and cold as Edna Thompson in thirty years?

David did not seem to share Amy's disillusionment. "That woman is a magnificent scholar," he said under his breath as Dr. Thompson left them. Amy nodded wordlessly and inched her way through the crowd to the buffet table. Loading a plate with hors d'oeuvres, she left David happily exchanging department gossip with a fellow professor and slipped out the door onto the patio. She sat down gingerly in a lawn chair and gazed into the Thompsons' garden.

"Bored with the party already?" Rick asked blandly as he sat down beside her. His plate was piled as high as hers.

"It's—stuffy in there," Amy stammered, twisting her little ring. What could she say? That she was disappointed in Mrs. Thompson? Curious, she turned to Rick. "How well do you know Dr. Thompson?" she asked.

"Quite well," Rick admitted. "He is my godfather. He is an old friend of my mother's, and to a lesser extent of my father's as well. Dr. Thompson's been like an uncle to me."

"I thought you might have been a former student or something like that," Amy said.

Rick snickered. "I don't think I have that kind of intellectual equipment." He laughed. To Amy's relief, he said it quite matter-of-factly, and not with the usual attitude of self-deprecation that many had around her.

"I think you've done just fine without it," Amy replied lightly, tapping the arm of the lawn chair with her forefinger.

"Yes, I have, but you couldn't convince some of them in there of that," Rick said quietly.

Amy could not answer that. Although she was not a snob about her intelligence, she knew that many of her fellow academics were, and more than once she had cringed at a superior remark about "the masses" or "the common mind." Rather then comment on Rick's statement, she chose to change the subject. "Are you shooting for me Sunday, or is one of the other photographers going?"

"I thought about sending Joe, but you two probably would be so busy gazing in rapture at each other—"

"Very cute!" Amy grimaced.

"—that you wouldn't get anything done. I'm making the sacrifice and taking you myself. What time do we leave?"

"About six?" asked Amy hesitantly.

Rick nodded, not objecting to the early hour. "We stay overnight and come back Monday evening. Or do you teach Monday morning?"

Amy shook her head. "I'm off Mondays. You know what to bring?"

Rick nodded his head. "I did something like this two years ago. Do we still share the cabin?" he asked innocently.

"Sure," Amy replied, suddenly not sure at all. The business arrangement that she had envisioned was quickly becoming a far more personal relationship, and she doubted the wisdom of sharing intimate quarters with Rick. But without making an issue of it, she had to stay in the cabin with him.

"Good," Rick said wickedly. "I thought that once you got to know me, you might change your mind."

"Not a chance," scoffed Amy bravely as she twisted the tiny ring. Rick looked at her hand and smiled.

"Discussing Amy's pictures?" David broke in as he joined them on the patio. "Really, Amy, you should be in there circulating. You don't get to party that often, you know."

"I'm fine out here, David," Amy said. She felt vaguely irritated at David's interruption, although she knew that he was right about her joining the party. "I don't believe you've met Rick yet. Rick Patterson, David Houston. Yes, David, Rick and I leave Sunday morning."

David turned to Rick and smiled, although his smile was a bit strained. "I'm so glad that you're taking Amy's pictures. Her book will be much better for having them."

"I understand that they are quite important to her work," Rick replied.

47

David shrugged. "Yes, I think so."

"So does Dr. Thompson," Rick said as he stood up. "David's right, Amy. You need to get in there and party." Rick took Amy's plate in one hand and helped her up with the other. "Lead on, pretty lady. And I do mean pretty," he whispered in her ear as David stiffened at the intimate gesture.

The party was in full swing. Amy and David quickly became separated from Rick and joined a group of rather stuffy teaching assistants and young professors discussing their summer plans. Several had secured jobs off-campus as lifeguards or waiters. Some were still hunting, rather desperately in a couple of cases, for some kind of job to help support a growing family. Some, like David and Amy, were teaching through the summer and continuing work on a research project. Although Amy had nothing against her colleagues and, in fact, enjoyed working with them, sometimes she wished that they could do more than talk shop, like tell dirty jokes. Have you heard the one about the traveling salesman . . . ?

"I wouldn't worry about summer work if I could get that associate professorship and the extra salary that goes with it," Jack Morgan, one of the newest teachers, volunteered. Jack had a wife and two children at home, and money was always tight at his house.

"Yeah," chimed in Ned Lewis, also a married man. "What I wouldn't give for that spot!"

If I told a dirty joke, I wonder if anyone would get it? Amy thought to herself.

"Needing and getting that one are two different things," David commented. "It's awarded strictly on merit."

"That's right." Amy nodded as she jerked her thoughts back to the discussion. "It doesn't matter whether or not the appointee needs the money. The appointment is made to the most qualified for the position." There! I said the right thing and didn't embarrass David. She wondered what David would do if she were to dance with a lampshade on her head.

48

"It's actually the fairest way to do it," David said blandly.

"I agree," Amy said wryly. "Sometimes achievement should be rewarded." Rick would probably love a dirty joke, she thought, and then became irritated for thinking about Rick again.

"Hear, hear," said Jack as he waved his drink in the air. "Spoken like a true scholar and the most probable appointee for the associate professorship." Several of the others nodded.

Amy shook her head. "I don't have a chance," she protested. "There are lots of other people who are more likely to get it than I am." But Amy admitted to herself that she would give a year's growth if she could get the position.

"False modesty is not becoming," Jack chided her. "Speaking of modesty, I'm glad you've finally dropped some of yours and dolled up for a change. Who was the fellow out on the patio who was enjoying the new Amy?"

"Rick Patterson," Amy said, embarrassed that she and Rick had been noticed. Had anyone jumped to any unfounded conclusions? Or better yet, had anyone jumped to any founded conclusions? "He's doing the pictures for my new book," she added swiftly.

"He could do more for me than just my pictures," commented Maureen, Jack's pretty wife. "That one is a doll if I ever saw one."

"I hear he's a gifted photographer as well," Ned added.

"I guess he's all right if you like the mindless arty types," David drawled.

Maureen Morgan stifled a gasp. A prickling sensation ran down Amy's spine, and she turned around in apprehension. Sure enough, Rick was standing right behind her and David and had heard every word. And with him stood Dr. Thompson.

Rick seemed unaffected, maybe even a little amused, by David's comment. Not so Dr. Thompson. His face turned red under the shock of white hair, and he obviously strove to contain his temper. Rick laid his hand on Dr. Thompson's arm. "Let it go," he said in a low voice. "Don't spoil your party."

David turned around and colored hotly when he saw Dr. Thompson standing beside Rick. Amy was mortified, remembering what Rick had said on the patio about what many intellectuals thought of him. What if Rick thought that she felt that way about him? After all, she and David were very close.

David turned to Rick and swallowed. "I hope you will accept my sincere apologies for a totally uncalled-for remark," he said quietly. "I meant nothing personal by it."

Rick smiled faintly. "I'm aware of that," he said sardonically.

"All the more reason for you not to say it," Dr. Thompson said between clenched teeth. "It's thoughtless remarks like that one that do the most damage sometimes." Amy was surprised by Dr. Thompson's vehemence. The remark had been unkind, but Dr. Thompson's anger seemed out of proportion to the incident.

"Don't get worked up, Harold," Rick said. Turning to David, he said, "Apology accepted. Think no more of it." Rick turned on his heels and strode away.

"At least he's gracious," said Jack Morgan. "And I'd say that one isn't so mindless." He shot a pointed look at David.

They stayed another two hours, but the party was spoiled for Amy. Deeply embarrassed by David's remark, she sat quietly in the corner, drumming her fingers absently on the sofa and sipping champagne. By the time David finally retrieved her from the corner, she had developed a nauseating headache. She managed to say her good-byes without letting on that she was uncomfortable and to negotiate the half block to David's car, sinking with relief into the seat. Her head was pounding and she hoped David would drive home quietly. Instead he seemed determined to dissect the party all the way home. Had she enjoyed herself? Wasn't Mrs. Thompson interesting? Had she liked the food? David seemed to be chattering to avoid the topic of Rick, but finally he broached the subject tentatively.

50

"Boy, I guess I blew it with Dr. Thompson with that comment about Rick. I had no idea that the old man was so touchy on the topic."

"Whatever possessed you to say such a cruel thing?" Amy asked a bit sharply. "You're usually much kinder than that."

"I don't know," David admitted. "Maybe jealousy."

"Jealousy?" Amy asked in bewilderment. "Why on earth would you be jealous of Rick?"

David shrugged his shoulders and smiled faintly as he turned off the freeway. "Normal male envy, I suppose. He's got the looks, that's for sure. With his talent he makes more money than you and I do together, and I'll just bet that he has an interesting social life. I wouldn't mind having those looks or that income."

"Do you envy him his social life, too?" Amy asked quietly.

"Oh, Amy, hon, of course not," David said quickly. "You know I think you're the greatest. Look, I'm sorry I spoiled the party for you."

He pulled up in front of her apartment, and she snapped open her car door and climbed out. "I'll call you tomorrow," David called to her, realizing that Amy was upset.

"Sure," Amy said through stiff lips. She unlocked her apartment and slammed the door behind her, then kicked off her shoes and sat down on the sofa. Why was she so upset? she asked herself. It was not the first time that David had made that kind of unthinking remark. Was she hurt this time because Rick had been the object of David's scorn? You bet you are, a little voice inside her taunted. You got all sensitive because David was talking about Rick. Watch it, Amy cautioned herself. You better remember where your loyalties should lie. David is the one in your future, not Rick.

Suddenly the future was not as interesting as it had been. The safe, predictable future with David seemed stifling tonight for some reason. Amy got up and wandered to the front door. Obeying a sudden impulse, she put on her shoes and left her apartment and walked up and down the sidewalk, her shoulders

51

hunched in thought. The soft warm breeze ruffled her hair, and a few stars twinkled above her head, bright enough to be seen through the city haze. She stared up at the twinkling stars and thought about her plans. Yes, David would provide well, he would be a faithful husband and father, and he would care about her in the best way that he knew how. A month ago that had seemed like enough, but was it now?

Amy wandered over to the porch swing that was suspended from a large oak tree and sat down in it, swinging back and forth in the soft air, the creaking of the swing soothing her frayed nerves. She thought about the party again. She could very easily find herself married to David and going to parties like that for the rest of her life. Yet, if she married him, the silly, impulsive side of her nature would have to be quelled for good. The parties would always be just like the one tonight, with everyone saying the right thing, doing the right thing. Could she stand that forever? Was that all there was for her?

Restlessly she got up and strolled up the sidewalk again, kicking a rock gently so as not to ruin the toe of her sandal. She wished she knew for sure that a future with David was the right thing for her. Up until tonight she had thought that it was, but now a burning indecision gripped her. If she didn't marry David, then what? Suddenly, for no reason whatsoever, Amy wondered what it would be like to be involved with Rick. Marriage? Impossible. Secure? Never. She would not know from one day to the next where she stood with him. But the times they were together would never be dull. Rick would never stand for a boring conversation at his party! He would do anything to liven it up! Amy's lips twitched as she thought of her traveling salesman joke. Rick would love it. She would have to be sure and tell it to him tomorrow.

Amy packed the last of her equipment and added it to the growing pile in the middle of the living room floor. Her clothes did not take up much room, but the diving gear took up a large canvas bag, and her collection bottles and preservatives filled two cardboard boxes. Rick had insisted on driving them up to the lake himself, arguing successfully that his van would be much more practical than the Nova to haul both his equipment and hers. Checking the clock on the wall, Amy shrieked and ran for the bathroom. Joe Valdez was due to pick her up in thirty minutes, so she could help him shoot a wedding. David had been disappointed that they could not go out, but he understood that she had a job to do.

Amy showered quickly and dried off in record time. She was rushing to her bedroom to find a set of clothes when the doorbell rang. Grabbing a terry cloth robe, she pulled it tight around her figure and opened the door a crack. Peeking out, she gasped to see not macho Joe, but Rick's grinning face peering back at her through the door. His grin faded, however, when he noted her state of dishabille.

"Good God, woman, we have a wedding to shoot! Aren't you ready yet?"

"You're not Joe," Amy said unreasonably as she opened the door to admit him. "Besides, you're early."

"Not that early," Rick ground out. "Go get ready."

Amy smothered the retort that sprang to her lips. Conscious of the thinness of the terry robe, she fled to the bedroom and slipped into underwear and a cool blue sweater dress. Betty Jean had advised her to dress for a wedding as though she were a wedding guest. She would be less conspicuous in the crowd and would not run the risk of offending anyone who felt that casual clothing was out of place at a wedding. Amy fumbled her way into a pair of panty hose and some shoes and fairly ran back to the bathroom. As she passed the living room Rick called out, "Hurry up! We're getting later by the minute."

"Don't yell at me," Amy snapped. "That just makes me slower."

Deciding not to take time to dry her hair, Amy slicked the short wet locks behind her ears and secured them with two gold hairpins. She quickly made up her face and grabbed a purse from the closet. As she fumbled with her belongings, Rick reached out and took them from her. "I'll put what you need in the camera case," he said. "Your hands will be full tonight."

Amy handed him her keys and a comb. She started to add her lip gloss but by that time Rick had snapped the case shut and was striding out the door. Amy shut the door behind her and followed him to a snappy orange Datsun. He locked the camera case in the trunk and held the door for Amy. The interior of the Datsun was not very large, and she could smell Rick's tangy after-shave and feel the heat radiate from his body.

"You look lovely in the dress and makeup," Rick commented. Amy sniffed, still put out at having been rushed. "But I like you better without them," Rick continued smoothly.

Amy looked over at him. He was grinning again, watching embarrassment steal across her expressive face. "Do you always say outrageous things like that?" she snapped.

"No, only when the lady in question answers the door in a sexy robe," he replied wickedly.

Oh, no, was the robe that thin? How much had he seen? Unconsciously Amy ran her hand down her chest between her breasts. Determined to make the most of the moment, Rick said, "Not there, pretty lady. You had your back to me, remember?"

"Where's Joe?" Amy broke in quickly to distract Rick from any more teasing. Her face was burning and she had the silly urge to cover her bottom with her hands. She sneaked a look at Rick and had to stifle the urge to wipe the smug expression off his face. He knew that he had got to her again!

"Why? Think you would have been safer with him?" Rick asked as he pulled the Datsun onto the expressway.

"Yes, I do," Amy retorted with spirit, tapping the car seat with her finger.

"Sorry about that," Rick said unrepentantly. "Betty Jean booked a last-minute wedding for a friend of Joe's and they asked

Joe to do it. Frankly, I don't shoot that many myself anymore. I'm tired of them."

"How many have you shot in all?" Amy asked curiously.

"Over two thousand," Rick admitted.

"Two thousand! No wonder you're tired of them."

"Has anyone explained to you what your duties are tonight?" Rick asked as he snapped on the blinker and took a cloverleaf, heading downtown.

"No," Amy replied. "Betty Jean said that Joe would explain it all to me when he picked me up."

"Well, your duties will be many and varied, and if you do them right, you'll be a lot of help to me." Gone was the teasing flirt. Rick was now completely businesslike. "The first pictures I shoot are of the bridal party—the bride with her mother, the attendants, and so on. Here you hand out flowers, straighten trains and veils if necessary, find the next people who are to be photographed, and mostly keep back everyone who isn't in the picture. Got that so far?"

Amy carefully repeated her instructions, ticking off each point on her fingers.

"Smart lady," Rick commented as he took a downtown exit. "Next, you save me an aisle seat in the back of the church while I go shoot the groom and his attendants." At Amy's raised eyebrow he added, "You might cramp my style out there. I take care of everything during the wedding. After the ceremony, we shoot the group pictures. Here's a list of the pictures I usually take." He reached into his jacket and handed her a short list. "Have these people seated in order in the front pew. That way they're ready when I call for them. Oh, I don't permit any other photographs to be taken until I'm through, so tell them to put their Instamatics away." Amy nodded.

"At the reception I ad-lib a lot. You can relax a little and get a plate of food, but keep an ear open and be ready when it's time for the bouquet and the garter. I use a second strobe on those shots." He drove through the narrow congested downtown streets toward an old Protestant church. "When those pictures are taken, your job is officially over, although I usually stay to shoot the dramatic exit." Rick turned the Datsun into a city parking garage and parked on an upper level. He fished his camera bag out of the trunk and casually took Amy's hand as they walked down the stairs into the warm summer evening.

Amy hoped Rick did not notice the slight trembling of her fingers. Just the touch of her hand in his awakened a restless longing in her. She tried to convince herself that her feelings were caused by the soft summer air and the romantic old city, but she was too smart a lady to lie to herself. You're attracted to him, she thought. It isn't the night or the city. You would be attracted to him anytime, anywhere.

Rick walked silently beside her, not releasing her hand. Together they crossed an old curved bridge spanning the San Antonio River and took a shortcut through La Villita, the beautifully restored little village that was now a collection of exclusive boutiques. They crossed a wide thoroughfare and hurried up the steps of the old brick church where the wedding was to take place. When Rick let go of her hand in the vestibule, Amy experienced an unreasonable sense of loss.

The next two hours were a revelation to Amy. She had been to her share of weddings, but she had always been a guest and seen the finished product only. This was the first time she had been behind the scenes.

They found the nervous young bride and her party in a state of pandemonium in the ladies' lounge in the back of the church. The bride was from one of San Antonio's most prominent families, and the groom was from an equally illustrious Houston clan. Money was in evidence in the dresses, the flowers, the bride's huge diamond solitaire, and the fact that they had hired Patterson's Pics. Rick popped out a camera and called for the bride and her bridesmaids. As quickly as she could, Amy located the florist's box of bouquets and handed one quickly to each bridesmaid, then gave the small basket to the flower girl, who was sulking in the corner. Next she located the corsages for each mother and helped pin them on, sticking her finger twice and drawing blood the second time, although she was too rushed to even notice the injury. Meanwhile Rick was shooting pictures of the bride alone, the bride with her giggling bridesmaids, the bride with her nervous mother, and the bride with her sullen soon-to-be mother-in-law.

Amy felt herself becoming caught up in the pandemonium and marveled at the patience Rick exhibited with the women. To him this was undoubtedly just another job, but this was an important event in the lives of these people, and Rick managed to reflect their excitement yet take his pictures quickly and skillfully. Amy coaxed the pouting flower girl to smile for Rick and kiss the bride, and so felt that she had done a little to help. Then, as suddenly as it had begun, the pandemonium died down. The pictures were finished.

Wearily Amy carried herself to the sanctuary, relieved that she could sit down for a few minutes. She looked down at her fashionably high heels and promised herself to wear medium heels next time, and to be more careful around the corsages. That finger hurt! She held an aisle seat for Rick as he had asked her to and listened to the quiet organ, watching as obviously wealthy guests filed in on the arms of the ushers. The large church was filling rapidly, and Amy correctly assumed that the guest list had been a long one. Would she and David have a large wedding? Probably not. David considered a lot of pomp and ceremony ridiculous, and on their incomes he was probably right. They would most likely marry quietly in the university chapel. But as she watched the ushers light the tapering rows of candles, she was conscious of a sharp sense of disappointment. She would love to have a fancy wedding like this one, to take her vows in a long lace dress in white, and to dance away the night at a lavish reception. She sighed softly. David would never go along with it, so she better shelve all those dreams now. But a wedding is

57

a small thing, she reminded herself. The important thing is the man and the marriage.

Rick slid into the aisle seat beside Amy and quickly changed the film in the camera. His face was a combination of exasperation and unholy amusement. "Groom's drunk," he whispered.

"Oh, no!" gasped Amy, horrified.

"Shh!" whispered Rick. "And don't be too surprised. Happens all the time. Just makes my job harder, that's all."

"But what will they do?" asked Amy.

"They're back there sobering him up a little with some coffee. Don't worry, they won't call off the wedding."

Amy watched the ceremony in fascination, fully expecting the groom to reveal his state of intoxication to the entire church. The groom, a handsome young blond, appeared normal except for a slight thickening of his speech that Amy would have attributed to nerves if she had not known better. The rest of the ceremony was beautiful.

Leaning over to whisper a comment to Rick, she was surprised to find the aisle seat empty beside her. She searched the darkened room with her eyes and finally spotted him standing unobtrusively to one side of the altar, shooting available-light pictures of the ceremony in progress. He made no noise and could hardly be seen in the dim sanctuary. Amy watched him until he silently slipped back up the aisle and out the back door, then she returned her attention to the bridal couple. She did not hear Rick enter the sanctuary, but by the time the ceremony was finished he was sitting beside her again. He snapped a quick shot of the now radiant bride and the bemused groom as they came back up the aisle.

The group pictures were another exercise in pandemonium. As soon as the church was empty Amy and Rick corralled the wedding party and assorted relatives and herded them back into the sanctuary. Suddenly Rick was no longer a discrete observer, but was completely in charge of the proceedings. Politely but firmly he called for the wedding party while Amy arranged the relatives in the pew in the proper order according to her list. Rick posed the entire wedding party in front of the altar and took several group shots. Then, dissatisfied, he handed Amy a strobe and stood her on the front pew, aiming the auxiliary strobe at the bride and groom. Unfortunately, at this point the groom began to sway and was prevented from falling only by the combined efforts of the bride and the best man. Rick's snapped orders sent a distant cousin in search of another cup of coffee, and a glaring scowl from Rick inspired the groom to stay on his feet a little longer. Working as quickly as he could, Rick took all the family pictures and several poses of just the bride and groom together. Finally a steaming cup of coffee arrived, and thus fortified, the groom escorted his bride to their reception in the church banquet hall, where he proceeded to shake hands vigorously and extol his bride as the "purtiest little filly in Texas." Amy sat in the corner and by a magnificent act of will managed to not laugh out loud.

Rick moved through the crowd, taking candid shots of the guests. He managed to persuade the groom to stop shaking hands long enough to cut the cake, and before too much time had passed the bride's mother suggested that perhaps they would like to throw the bouquet and go. Before her new son-in-law disgraces himself any further, Amy thought as she caught the frantic look in the woman's eyes. Smiling blandly, Rick arranged the shots with Amy's help and took a picture of the youngest bridesmaid clinging proudly to the bride's bouquet. With much whistling and stomping and a ribald remark or two about the coming night, the garter was removed and thrown quite deliberately to the best man, then the bride's mother hustled the couple into the back to change. With sighs of relief, they left in a shower of rice and confetti.

Rick graciously accepted the thanks of the bride's parents, and with an expressionless face he packed his equipment. Amy strove to keep her face equally impassive as they said their good-byes and left the banquet hall. Walking at a brisk but steady pace, they rounded a corner and walked behind a tall building. Rick glanced over his shoulder, and seeing no one from the wedding, allowed his face to split into a wide smile. Then as he slowly released the tight rein that he had kept on his sense of humor, he started to laugh. He leaned against the side of the building and shook until tears ran out of his eyes. "Purtiest little filly in Texas!" Rick said as he laughed out loud.

Amy gave way to the laughter that she too had stifled all evening. She giggled as she thought of the groom's near collapse during the picture session and the way the harassed mother of the bride had hurried the couple out of the church. Passersby stared at Rick and Amy as though the two of them had lost their senses, but it was a number of minutes before either of them could stop laughing. "You know, we have a cruel sense of humor," she choked, holding her aching sides.

"I really feel sorry for that girl," Rick said as he shouldered his camera bag. "I'm afraid she's going to sleep like a baby tonight."

"And have to nurse an even bigger one tomorrow," Amy continued. "That has to be the funniest thing I've seen in a long time."

"That was mild," Rick said as they walked back toward the car. He retraced their route as far as the bridge, then Rick took her arm and steered her gently down the steps onto the Riverwalk. "I beat you out of supper earlier," he said. "I'll feed you some now." Amy started to point out that they had to leave in the morning by six, then decided that it would probably do no good. Rick had decided that they would eat. And she was hungry.

Rick selected a small Mexican restaurant with outdoor tables right on the water. As they demolished a plate of nachos, he entertained her with stories from the many weddings he had shot over the years. Amy laughed out loud at his stories about the bride whose zipper popped during the ceremony, the tall bride who could kiss the top of the groom's bald head, and the groom who was so intoxicated that he responded "Yup!" to the traditional question. In a more serious vein, Rick told her of the wedding ceremony that had been performed entirely in sign language because both the bride and the groom were deaf, and of the touching ceremony he had shot last year of a wheelchair couple. Conversation lagged as they both waded through an enchilada plate and washed it down with rich imported beer, but picked up again with Rick's story of the man who had liked Rick's work so much that he had hired Patterson's Pics to shoot all three of his weddings.

"Do you get much return business like that?" Amy asked curiously.

"Some," Rick admitted. "Or sometimes the marriage is over by the time we have the pictures ready to deliver. And then there is the occasional couple that is a threesome by the time the order is ready."

"Can you tell at the wedding when something like that is going to happen?" asked Amy, swallowing the last of her beer.

"Well, my observations are subjective, but, yes, I can frequently predict at the wedding whether or not a marriage is going to make it. Little things that I have noticed over the years seem to make a difference."

"How about the couple tonight?" Amy asked. "Do you think their marriage will last?"

"Hard to say," Rick said. "The fact that he felt the need to get drunk isn't really a good sign. But they did spend the evening together. Usually couples who spend a good deal of the reception together have a better chance of making it than those who separate the minute they get in the door."

"I think the bride was holding him up," Amy said wryly.

"That may be so," Rick agreed. "The other good sign is that they left early. Most couples who are going to make it are in a hurry to be alone together. If they want to stay all night, they either don't care for each other's company or they're already living together."

"I got the feeling that Mama was in a hurry to get rid of sonny-boy." Amy laughed. "I guess it's been enough to make you cynical about marriage, hasn't it?"

"Who said I was cynical about marriage?" Rick asked sardonically.

"I'm sorry," Amy mumbled. "I thought since you've seen so much, and you're thirty-five and—"

"Thirty-six," Rick inserted.

"All right, you're thirty-six and you're not married yet. Or were you married before or something?"

"No," Rick said lightly as he handed the waiter a credit card. "I've never been married, but I certainly have nothing against the institution. I fully intend to marry someday."

"Why haven't you married before now?" Amy asked, fumbling for her purse before she remembered that she had not brought one.

"Yes, I know," Rick said as he pocketed the credit card the waiter handed him and stood up. "What's taking me so long?" He took Amy's arm and walked with her down the sidewalk skirting the river. Tasteful lighting made the walkway safe yet romantic rather than glittery, and laughter and music filtered out of the restaurants and taverns lining the Riverwalk. Amy breathed in the soft night air and unconsciously moved closer to Rick as the pathway narrowed.

"Well," she said quietly, "what's taking you so long?"

Rick picked up the thread of the conversation they had been sharing at the restaurant. "I haven't met the right woman yet. I've known many lovely women over the years and loved more than one of them, but I've never met one interesting enough to keep me satisfied for the rest of my life."

Amy stared at him, astonished. "Why, Rick Patterson, I do believe you are a romantic!"

"Not at all," Rick replied, showing no sign of embarrassment at having revealed his feelings so completely. "I can think of no other basis for a lasting marriage. How about you? What's taking you so long?"

"I loved somebody once," Amy admitted. "He hurt me badly. For a long time I wasn't sure what I wanted in a relationship."

"What did you finally decide to base your next relationship on?" Rick asked.

What will I base it on, or what would I like to base it on? Amy said to herself. Aloud she said, "I guess I'd like the same thing you would. Common interests, similar professional goals, maybe a joint career."

Rick laughed out loud. "You call that satisfying? You think that's what I want in a marriage? I could give a damn what she does for a living! I meant that I want a woman who can interest me as a woman and satisfy me as a man. Someone to talk to, to laugh with, to make love to, to have babies with."

"That's all you want?" Amy asked primly. "A sexual companion?"

"No, that's hardly all I want, although that sure as hell is important." Rick's voice sounded irritated. "How about you? You and that redheaded scholar ever going to get out of the laboratory and into the bed together?" he taunted.

Amy sniffed. "I hardly think that's your concern. If David and I do marry, and at this point it looks as though we most probably will, we will have other planes of communication besides sexual. I fully expect that when everything else is right, the sex will come."

"Spoken like the dormitory virgin," Rick jeered. "If you two were right for each other, you would be communicating on that sexual plane as often as on any other. You and David have about as much appeal for each other as a couple of wet dishrags."

"What do you know about it?" Amy hissed. Rick was getting too close to the truth. "What the hell do you know about David and me?"

"I know that he can't touch you. You're unmoved by him, and

if you marry him, you're going to stay unmoved for the rest of your life, no matter how many times he takes your body."

"Then I guess it doesn't matter if I do marry him, because I'll never know the difference," Amy shot back, stung.

"Be damned if that's going to happen," Rick said as he jerked her to him. He backed off the sidewalk into the shadow of a curving bridge and swung Amy around and leaned her up against a vine-covered wall. "If you insist on marrying that jerk David, so be it, but you're going to go into it knowing what you're missing!" he spat savagely.

Amy opened her mouth to protest but the sound was cut off by the swift descent of Rick's mouth on hers. He kissed her violently, forcing her lips open wider and thrusting his hot tongue inside of her mouth. Amy stiffened momentarily at the unwanted invasion, but as her traitorous body began to respond her mouth welcomed him and her tongue began its own forays. Rick softened his kiss and pulled back to ease the pressure, then began rubbing his lips seductively against hers. Amy's hands crept up and wound their way into Rick's hair, and she applied enough pressure to force Rick's head closer to her own. Her mouth was tingling and she felt a tremor go through her body at the sensations that his mouth was creating. Dear Lord, he excited her!

Rick's hands slid down her back and settled around her tiny waist, spanning it with his fingers, then he let one hand move up until it closed gently over one small breast. He gently palmed the tiny sensitive nipple through the thin fabric of Amy's sweater until it sat up in his hand. Amy allowed her hands to slide lower, down his shoulders and powerful arms, marveling at the leashed strength she felt there. Not releasing her mouth, he slid his hand even further up and slowly unbuttoned her sweater, then slipped his hand in and touched her bare breast, tickling the other small bud until it too was erect.

Wanting to further the intimacy, Amy slid her hands around his hard waist, allowing them to meet at his back before she slid them daringly lower, past his belt, onto his hips, and she felt the strength of his response to her touch. She arched closer to his delightful fingers, forgetting everything but the lovely world of sensation that he was bringing to her, and she to him.

The blast of a police siren on the street overhead broke the spell. Rick released Amy's lips and he deftly buttoned her sweater before allowing her to move. Amy stood motionless as turbulent feelings of passion gave way to rising shame. In truth, David had never made her feel even a tiny fraction of the passion that Rick had just casually made rise in her, and probably David never would. Looking at Rick with haunted eyes, she whispered brokenly, "Why did you do that?"

"Well, how does he compare?" Rick muttered harshly, his breathing still ragged.

Anger flared in Amy. "About like Samantha," she jeered. "Or did you do it on a waterbed with Linda this week?"

Rick took a deep breath and pulled Amy away from the side of the building. "Come on," he said tiredly. "I'm taking you home."

CHAPTER FOUR

Amy swore as she reached out her hand and swatted off the buzzing alarm. A virtually sleepless night had taken its toll and her head felt muzzy. Rubbing her gritty eyes, she groaned as she swung her legs over the side of the bed and stumbled toward the bathroom. Rick was due to pick her up in thirty minutes for their excursion to the first lakes they would visit this summer. Amy had never felt less like facing anyone in her life, but she had no doubt that if she tried to squirm out of the deal, Rick would personally carry her to the lake and take her pictures, with or without her cooperation.

Amy ran the water as hot as she could stand it, then crawled under the shower and let the hot stream pour over her still sensitive breasts and run down her body. She absently squirted shampoo into her hair as she relived Rick's devastating assault of the night before, although in all honesty it had been anything but assault. Amy had responded to Rick, both physically and emotionally, even as her mind had protested the propriety of her response. She ran her hand down her breasts and felt them rise in memory of his touch.

Amy was frankly baffled by Rick's behavior. She could not

understand his violent objection to her plans to marry David or his disgust with her reasons for doing so. It was as though he had a personal stake in her future, when in actuality nothing could be farther from the truth. Amy thought briefly that Rick might be jealous of her relationship with David, but almost immediately thrust that thought from her mind. With both Samantha and Linda to keep him satisfied, he had no need to be jealous of her.

Dressed in a T-shirt, a pair of cutoffs, and sneakers, face totally devoid of makeup, Amy was waiting at the door with a cup of instant coffee for Rick when he arrived five minutes early. He accepted the steaming mug with a nod of thanks and drank about half of it, then gestured to Amy's pile of supplies on the floor. "All this goes?" he asked.

Amy nodded. Wordlessly he picked up the canvas bag and one of the cartons of collecting jars and carried them out to his van. Amy followed with the other carton of bottles. The tension between the two of them was almost tangible. Looking at Rick in the early morning gloom, she remembered the feel of his mouth on hers under the bridge in the dark and her own mouth went dry with longing. Would Rick ever kiss her again, as her body and her emotions wanted him to, or had he accomplished his objective, whatever that was, last night? She followed Rick back up the stairs and picked up her small suitcase. "Is that all?" Rick said curtly. Amy nodded. "Then let's go."

Amy crawled into the passenger seat and pulled the heavy door shut behind her. Rick switched on the engine and skillfully maneuvered the awkward vehicle through the deserted streets. If San Antonio ever resembled a ghost town, it did so early on Sunday morning. Rick drove through the empty streets and pulled onto the highway that would carry them up into the Hill Country and to the lakes where Amy had spent so much of the last two years. Rick did not ask for directions, and Amy did not break the brittle silence to offer any. She found the silence extremely awkward, but if Rick was uncomfortable, he did not show it outwardly. He switched on the radio and hummed along absently with the latest pop tunes.

Feigning nonchalance, Amy stared out the window at the rocky, cedar-covered hills that rolled into the distance. Usually Amy found the sunrise in the Hill Country food for the spirit, but this morning the glorious pink and orange sun took second place in Amy's thoughts, relegated to that spot by her turbulent and confused feelings for her companion. She certainly didn't admire him, she thought as she chewed on her fingernail. Not only was he seeing two women, but he was putting the make on her, too. Nor did she admire herself. As she remembered her wanton response of the night before, she felt somehow cheapened, especially since one of the other women involved was someone as nice as Samantha. Yet, if he tried to kiss her again, would she respond to him or would she turn him away?

They stopped for breakfast in Johnson City, home of former President Lyndon Johnson. Amy glanced down at her casual attire, but Rick muttered, "Don't worry—I look just as bad," as he took her hand and led her into a small restaurant that was just opening. If the hostess was in any way offended by the cutoffs Amy and Rick were wearing, she did not show it. In fact, the woman openly admired Rick's tanned, muscular legs and chest as revealed by his shorts and thin cotton T-shirt, causing irritated jealousy to surge through Amy. What right did any man have to be so attractive? And what right did that give him to play around with her as he had last night?

Breakfast conversation was strained. Rick made a few attempts to talk to Amy, but she answered him in monosyllables and tackled her huge breakfast gratefully as an excuse not to talk. Rick watched first in amusement and then in amazement as Amy ate a breakfast equal to his and then asked him for his extra pieces of toast. She relaxed a little over a second cup of coffee, but her tension returned as the waitress brought the check and Amy withdrew her wallet from her pocket. She handed Rick enough money for her breakfast and part of the tip, but he abruptly shoved her money back across the table and got out a credit card. Fully aware that Rick was not above making a scene in the restaurant, Amy pocketed the money until they had left the restaurant but handed it to Rick in the van. "I want to pay for my share of breakfast," Amy protested.

"I always pay when I take out a lady," Rick said gruffly as he started the engine.

"But I'm not a lady!" Amy protested hotly, clenching her fist. "Well, I mean—" she stammered, "I mean this isn't a date or anything like that. It's a business deal, and I don't want to be beholden any more than I have to."

That seemed to make Rick angry. "You don't need to feel beholden for a three dollar breakfast," he snapped, handing the money back to Amy.

With shaking fingers, she tried to put the money back in her wallet and dropped the change all over the floor. In an attempt to rescue her money, Amy dived after it and soundly bumped heads with Rick, who had also ducked down to pick up the coins. Swearing softly, he turned off the engine and picked up the money while Amy sat in the corner, nursing her sore head. He placed the money in her wallet, then reached out and pulled Amy across the seat. She tried to slide away, but Rick's iron grip held her fast. He turned her so that her face was just a few inches from his and spoke to her slowly and gravely, but with that devilish humor in his eyes.

"You're just as nervous as a cat because of what I did to you last night," he said softly, "and you're half wanting me to do it again. I'm not going to apologize for kissing you last night, because you needed to be kissed. And furthermore, I intend to kiss you often, every time you need it. So you can stop worrying about if and when I plan to do it again. Because 'if' is 'yes,' and 'when' is 'right now'."

Amy stared mesmerized as Rick's head dipped and his mouth came down on her own. His lips were warm and seductive, with none of the burning anger they had held the night before. Mindlessly Amy melted against him, inching closer to his warm hard chest and curling her fingers around his broad shoulders. Rick briefly sampled the softness of her mouth and then pulled away, kissing each cheek gently and pulling her head against his shoulder. He held her cradled in his arms for long moments. Amy felt her body relaxing against the hard warmth of his. "Now," his voice rumbled in her ear, "will you stop acting like a nervous teenager around me?"

"I am not acting like a nervous teenager!" Amy snapped.

"That's more like it," Rick replied. Surprisingly the tension between them had vanished. "Then, until next time . . ." Rick said as he kissed her again.

Released from her nervousness, Amy talked to Rick all the way to the lake. They planned to visit Inks Lake first, since it was the smallest lake in the chain and the least important to Amy's study, and go from there to start work on Lake LBJ. The bulk of Amy's studies had been made on Buchanan Lake and its tributaries, and the majority of the pictures would be taken there at a later date. As she did at times, Amy chattered for the better part of an hour about her project, led on by Rick's interested questions. Obviously he did not know much about the scientific theory behind her work, but his technical questions were surprisingly astute, and he even made one or two excellent suggestions on how she could improve her collecting technique.

As they neared Dr. Thompson's small cabin Amy felt the familiar excitement she always experienced whenever she visited the lakes. Her feelings were in part due to the enthusiasm she felt for her research, but something in Amy's spirit responded to the clear cool waters and the rugged hillsides surrounding them. Rick drove the narrow trail to the cabin with such familiarity that Amy guessed correctly that he had visited here many times before. Situated on the waterfront of Buchanan Lake, the cabin was actually convenient to all three lakes in the chain.

Rick parked his van in the dirt track in front of the house and unlocked the front door. While Amy unloaded the food and suitcases, Rick hitched the small motor boat's trailer to the back of the van and loaded his and Amy's equipment into the boat, securing it firmly in a sealed compartment under the seat. Amy smiled appreciatively at Rick when she realized that he had just completed her most onerous chore.

"You usually do this alone?" Rick asked as he accepted a cold glass of water from her.

Amy nodded. "Yes, I know, it's too much for a small person like me." She rolled her eyes in mock disgust. "I'm supposed to be weak and helpless. Seriously, though, it was nice to have some help for a change."

"David doesn't come and help you?" Rick inquired.

"He used to come all the time," Amy said. "But he got caught up in his own project and hasn't had the time lately, so I've been doing it alone."

"It seems like he could get up here sometimes," Rick said tartly. His lips thinned and he said no more as he went into the house to change.

Soon, armed with lunch in an ice chest and wearing bathing suits under their clothes, Amy and Rick were lowering the motor boat into Inks Lake. Compared to the other two lakes in the study, Inks was not much more than a wide spot in the river, and Amy had not found the parasites to be much of a problem to the already scant population of mussels in the small lake. She took command of the boat and guided them up a small cove to where the sheltered waters gently lapped the sand. Amy tied the boat to a tree trunk and unselfconsciously stripped off her shorts and shirt to reveal her tan, slender body clad only in a string bikini. So intent was she on inspecting the mussel bed, she was totally unaware of the effect her near nudity had on Rick. He stared in stunned appreciation as her dainty, lithe form hopped over the side of the boat and slid into the green water.

Amy meticulously examined the mussel bed, starting in knee-high water and gradually working her way deeper until the water was as high as her breasts. Rick threw Amy a pair of goggles, and she donned them and continued her exploration. Finally satisfied, she swam back to the boat and bobbed her head over the side. "I'm ready to show you the pictures I need here," she said, and then stammered, "Come on," as she took in the sight of Rick's almost naked body. Like her, he had shed his shirt and shorts, and his brief blue swimsuit hid nothing of his wide, hair-covered chest or the bulging muscles in his arms and thighs. Amy stared dry-mouthed at the blatantly masculine form in front of her, and unwillingly she felt the urge to get as close to his body as she could. It would be heaven to run her fingers through the cloud of dark hair on his chest and feel the hard muscles beneath it. For the first time she was aware of her own near naked state. Mercifully she had no more time to dwell on his body or her own, since Rick promptly flipped into the water, two cameras strapped securely around his neck.

"Your cameras!" Amy gasped as they hit the water.

"They're waterproof," Rick said, laughing, as he deliberately dunked one of them in the green lake. "I use these for all my underwater work, as well as any dusty location shooting or any riot work. Now, pretty lady, show me what pictures you want."

They spent the better part of an hour in the muddy mussel bed, taking various shots of the bed itself and some of the individual mussels in the sandy shallows. Rick admitted that he had never actually seen live mussels before, in spite of the many times he had collected their shells on the lake shores. Amy pulled several out of the bed and showed them to Rick, demonstrating with a twig the strength with which a mussel could snap shut its shells. Amy then returned the mussels to the water, and she and Rick laughed together at the sight of the small creatures swiftly digging their way back into the sand.

When Rick felt that he had captured on film the pictures that Amy needed, they visited two more mussel beds, taking photographs and checking the beds for any parasite infestation. By that time it was after noon and breakfast had worn off long ago, so Amy steered the boat into a deserted cove and served her simple lunch to Rick. They attacked the sandwiches and chips like two starving prisoners, and Rick watched in amazement as Amy devoured as many sandwiches as he did. They washed down the sandwiches with iced tea, then Amy packed the hamper, and they returned to the boat dock.

Amy sat silently as Rick drove the few miles to Lake LBJ, drumming her fingers on the windowsill in time with the radio. In the enclosed van she was once again aware of the sensual appeal of Rick's body. He had put on his shorts over his suit, but he had not put on his shirt, and Amy had to fight an urge to run her fingers down his muscled side and around his waist. She had donned both her shirt and her shorts, not so much for modesty's sake but because the bikini, so practical in the water, was decidedly impractical out of it. Idly she wondered how a photographer who led only a moderately active life managed to stay in such peak physical condition. Although Rick was a large man, he had not an ounce of spare flesh on him, and tight muscles rippled in his stomach and his hips. Caught gazing at him, Amy stared coolly for a moment longer and looked out the opposite window, fuming silently when Rick chuckled softly.

The sailors and skiers were competing for space on Lake LBJ, and Amy very gingerly steered the small boat through the crowded water to the first mussel bed she wanted to visit. After the relative seclusion of Inks, the company they had on this lake was distinctly annoying. The first mussel bed that Amy approached was occupied by a group of boats anchored together having an impromptu party, and Amy swore under her breath and headed for the next cove.

This cove was occupied by a single boat that appeared deserted but that on closer examination was inhabited by a single pair of lovers, lying fast asleep on the hull of the luxury cruiser. Amy tied her boat far enough away from the larger one to provide some privacy and examined the mussel bed as she had the ones at Inks. Here the population had thinned out considerably since her last visit several weeks earlier, and she grimly recorded the changes in her notebook as Rick took pictures of the diminished population. Amy collected several live but sick mussels to take back with her for treatment.

Amy finished her work and sat in the boat, dispirited by her grim discovery. She watched as Rick completed the shots she had requested. He was truly a master at his craft, as much at home shooting pictures on a muddy beach as at a wealthy wedding. After finishing his work Rick climbed back into the boat and swiftly changed his film and stored the exposed roll in a waterproof pouch. Seeing Amy's dejected face, he ran his hand down her cheek and tilted her chin up to look at him. "Don't take it so hard," he chided gently. "Your medicine will save the little beasties."

Amy nodded as she smiled wanly. "I know it's silly to feel that way about a bunch of animals that can't even bark, but I feel like they're mine. When I started the project two years ago, these beds were full. Now most of them look like this one." Briskly she shook her head. "We better try that other cove again."

At that moment a shout arose from the other boat. "Hey, you turkeys, find your own place to make love. We got here first!" Amy watched, mortified, as the young female occupant of the other boat turned over, exposing her full breasts to the sun.

Rick laughed derisively as he pushed Amy away from the engine and started it himself. He swung the small boat around and passed right by the cruiser. Waving impudently at the other couple, he blasted out of the cove and on to the main body of the lake. "I'm not sure what that guy was sore about," Rick yelled in Amy's ear. "I was just enjoying the scenery."

Amy sniffed and looked away. Surreptitiously she glanced down at her small, flat chest and felt the old, familiar sense of inadequacy. In an age when the Playboy Bunny reigned supreme, Amy's small bosom was a source of embarrassment to her. She had developed late and had been the last girl in gym class to wear a bra, and still she was very small. During school

74

she had endured taunts of "Peter Pan" and "peanut chest," and she had naturally assumed that men found her lacking in that department. She knew intellectually that she was much too sensitive about being flat-chested, but that didn't stop the basic dissatisfaction she felt about her breasts. It seemed unfair to her that so many had so much, and that she had to hunt for a bra that was small enough. What seemed even more unfair was the importance attached to that particular attribute. Just look at Rick's reaction! Typical.

She sat silently, her sparkle gone, until they approached the original cove, now deserted by the party boats. Quickly Amy flipped over the side and examined the mussel bed, noting the changes and recording them in the notebook. Curtly she told Rick what pictures she needed here and climbed back in the boat. Rick took the photographs and flipped over the side into the boat. He took her chin in his hand and tilted it up so he could see into her eyes. "Out with it," he demanded. "What made you sore?"

Stubbornly Amy shook her head. "Nothing's wrong," she lied.

"Bull," Rick returned forcefully. "One minute you're happy as a lark and the next you're sulking. Did that idiot on the other boat get to you or something?"

"No," Amy replied shortly. "He didn't." She said nothing more.

"You know, I'm not going to let it go until you tell me what the hell's wrong, so why don't you come on out with it and get it over with?"

"All right," Amy said through clenched teeth. "Did you have to admire the scenery so much? Did you have to drool over that fabulous set she had? Do you have any idea how it feels to have men look right through you as if you weren't there? How would you like your dates to stare while a kid like her bounces through a restaurant?" Amy took a deep breath. "I'm sorry," she said simply. "I'm flat. It's always bothered me. I'm plain and I'm skinny to boot. It hurts, that's all. I didn't mean to take it out on you. Go ahead and enjoy the scenery."

Rick regarded her solemnly for a moment. Unwittingly she had just revealed a vulnerable side of herself, and she cringed when she realized just how ridiculous she must have sounded. Rick released her chin but took her face in his hands and examined it carefully, then studied her near naked body in the string bikini. Finally he set her away from him and picked up a camera. Before Amy could protest, he shot several pictures of her sitting in the boat, free of makeup and with wet hair and a sunburned nose. "Why did you do that?" Amy asked peevishly.

"I'm going to develop these, and I'm going to show them to you," he said. "And I'm going to take more. I'm going to show you what fabulous bones you have in your face and what graceful lines you have in your body. I'm sorry that you feel skinny and plain, because nothing could be further from the truth. No, your beauty is not showy, and no, you're not voluptuous, but I think that when you're sixty and your face is still beautiful, you won't mind so much not being exotic. Besides, she's going to sag after a couple of kids, while those exquisite little breasts of yours are only going to get better."

Amy stared down in amazement at Rick's intimate appraisal of her face and body. "But David's never even noticed my looks," she said half to herself.

"Neither would your brother," Rick responded wryly. "But that doesn't mean that you don't have them. Take it from me. I'm an expert."

Amy's eyes widened, and then she realized that he meant professionally. At least she hoped he did.

Amy selfishly claimed the first shower back at the cabin. While Rick unloaded their equipment and unhitched the trailer, she rinsed away the fishy smell and put on a fresh pair of shorts and a shirt. Studying her face in the mirror, she tried to see herself the way Rick had described her and failed, although she had to admit that she had never appreciated her small, even features. Rick's comments about her breasts were outrageous, yet a warm feeling that she had never had about her body settled around her. Did Rick, in fact, mean what he said, or did he just want to make her feel better? She could not answer that, and she did not think that Rick would.

Amy prepared a simple supper of steaks and French fries while Rick showered. The bathroom was backed up to the kitchen, and Amy was amused and rather pleased to hear him singing decidedly off-key and splashing loudly. The noise from the shower stopped, and Rick wandered out, wearing only a towel around his waist. The towel actually revealed less than his swimsuit had, but Amy stared at him in fascination and splattered herself with hot grease. Her pained howl brought Rick running into the kitchen. "How on earth did you manage to do that?" he asked as he helped her wash off the hot grease.

"I wasn't watching what I was doing," Amy admitted as she hurriedly turned her face back to the cooking.

"See where peeking will get you?" Rick asked wickedly.

"Oh, go put on some clothes!" Amy snapped, furious that Rick should have guessed so accurately the reason that she burned herself.

Laughing, Rick pulled a pair of clean cutoffs and another T-shirt from his suitcase and went in the bathroom to change. Suddenly Amy realized that they were actually going to share a very small cabin and that privacy would be at a minimum. Dr. Thompson had never suggested that other arrangements be made for Rick, and Amy had honestly thought at the beginning that their relationship would be platonic and that sharing the cabin would be no problem. But their relationship was hardly platonic, and they still had no choice but to share quarters. How on earth would they manage? Amy wondered. There were two small bedrooms, but since these were so hot, Amy usually slept on one of the daybeds in the main room when she was alone. Now she guessed that she would have to sleep in one of the small

77

bedrooms and that Rick would take the other. They would be hot, but there was really no other choice.

Dressed in the clothes he had taken with him into the bathroom, Rick came back into the kitchen with a tube of burn ointment. Wordlessly Amy extended her arm and winced as Rick touched the tender spots with the soothing cream. When the burns were tended, he recapped the tube and rummaged around in the refrigerator. He found a bag of spinach and some cucumbers that Amy had not brought. "Mind if I make my favorite salad?" he asked as he ripped open the bag.

"Be my guest," Amy said sincerely. Rick washed the spinach over the sink and let it drain while he peeled the cucumbers. She watched him as he sliced them and then went to work on the spinach. He knows his way around the kitchen, she thought. But David did too, she reminded herself firmly.

Rick and Amy worked together in comfortable silence, with no "you do this and I'll do that," and before too long they put supper on the small dining table. As an added touch, Rick found a bottle of red wine in the refrigerator and uncorked it for them to share. They talked about everything under the sun while they packed away their steaks and fries, and Amy took two helpings of Rick's delicious salad. He finally pushed his plate away, declaring himself full, but Amy got out a carton of ice cream and dished up a large bowl.

"Hey, I said I was full," Rick protested.

"I know," Amy said calmly. "This is for me."

"You're kidding!" Rick replied. "You're going to eat all that after that steak you just put away?"

"Of course," Amy said solemnly as she dug into the ice cream. Rick watched her eat part of it, then gathered up his plate and utensils and carried them into the kitchen. Amy followed in a few minutes with her own dishes and put them into the soapy water.

"Do you always eat like that?" Rick asked as Amy returned the ice-cream carton to the freezer.

"Like what? The local trucker? Sure do." Amy laughed as she picked up a dish towel and dried the dishes Rick had washed. "I used to be a lot worse. It used to embarrass poor Mother to death. She and Daddy would take me to stay with friends, and I'd ask what was for supper while we did the lunch dishes. I think I nearly broke my parents at the grocery store when I was a teenager."

"I didn't realize you had a family," Rick said in surprise.

"Why should you think a thing like that?" Amy retorted as she hung up the dish towel to dry.

Rick motioned Amy toward the door, and Amy nodded readily. "I didn't think you had a family because you had never mentioned them," he said as they walked toward the foaming water pounding the lakeshore. Buchanan Lake was larger than either of the two other lakes and would whitecap if the wind was high. The waves slapped the beach, bouncing off the sand with rhythmic regularity.

Amy stared out into the rolling waves and cocked her head to one side. "Then let me correct that omission right now," she said. "Perhaps I haven't mentioned my parents because they are so very special to me. My dad retired from his construction job several years ago and raises cattle on the ranch my mother inherited. She's a really super person—they both are. She worked hard to help my father put Marsha and me through school, and then when I wanted to go on, they paid for as much of it as they could. They helped Marsha and her husband when they first married. Marsha's a nurse—a good one. And she's really got the looks, but she doesn't realize that she's beautiful."

"Like someone else I know," Rick said quietly.

Amy ignored Rick's innuendo. She knew that he was trying to be kind, and she did not want him to patronize her. She smiled wistfully, wishing she could believe him. Continuing, she said, "I guess what I really love about my family is that they don't see me as different. They have always accepted me, brain and all, as being just like them. If I mess up, they tease me, and if I do well, they are glad, but they're comfortable around me at the same time."

"And other people aren't?" Rick asked quietly. "Are you really so different?"

Amy considered the question. "I don't think I'm so different," she said, "but sometimes other people do. And, no, most people aren't comfortable around me, at least they aren't after they find about this." She tapped her forehead with her finger.

"How can you say that?" Rick challenged. "The office staff loves you. You've done fine with them."

"So I have," Amy admitted. "But then they don't know too much about my academic career. And remember, they aren't competing with me for a grade or a scholarship or a job."

Rick laid his arm across her shoulders as he guided her back toward the cabin. The sun was down and a brilliant full moon peeked out from behind thin clouds. The lights from the dam winked across the shimmering water. "I wouldn't worry so much about others accepting you," Rick said gently. "A lot of your feelings are left over from the days when you were beating them out of their grade point curves. You haven't been doing that for some time. I think if you will just relax and let them, other people will accept you just like your family does."

"I wish I could believe you," Amy said wistfully as she opened the front door.

"You can," Rick said confidently. "I know someone who's a whole lot like you, and it worked out for her. Now, I want to develop the black and white I took today, and I know you want to get your notes together. I need the kitchen for a while, so get anything you need out of there before I start."

Amy did not want anything out of the kitchen, so she gathered up the roughly scratched notes and stretched out on one of the daybeds in the main room. Rick disappeared into the kitchen with several large trays and a large red light and locked the door behind him. Amy tried to make sense of her notes, but the sleeplessness of the night before and the busy day she had just put in took their inevitable toll, and before she had sorted out the first page of her notes, her eyes had closed and she was asleep.

A scratching sound at the screen drew Amy from drugged slumber. Sitting up slowly, she threw aside a thin sheet and wondered why she was still in her clothes when she always wore a nightgown to bed. The scratching at the screen continued, causing Amy to purse her lips in exasperation and stumble to the kitchen. Mumbling under her breath, she poured a saucer of milk and tore open a packet of cat food. She opened the screen door and shoved the midnight snack out on the porch. "There you go, you hungry so-and-so," she said in mock irritation.

Scratching her sunburned neck, Amy decided that a night-gown would be more comfortable than her shorts and top. She groped for her suitcase in the dark and snapped it open, with-drawing a thin cotton gown. She stripped off her clothes and kicked them across the floor, then reached up to pull the night-gown over her head. As she writhed into the nightgown she stubbed her toe on the daybed and uttered a sharp curse.

"Damn, woman, I could forgive the cat, but do you have to make so much noise?"

Amy jumped and stubbed her toe again. She whirled around in the direction of the irate voice to confront Rick's scowling face. Lounging on the other daybed, he was covered only with a sheet that had slid down around his flat stomach, and in the poor light Amy could not tell whether he wore anything besides the sheet to sleep in. Looking behind her, she realized that the full moon had fallen across her nude body as she had stripped off her shorts and shirt, and she realized that Rick had seen her naked. Standing paralyzed in mortification, she jumped when Rick snapped on the lamp behind his daybed. Involuntarily her eyes looked into his sleepy face, noting that the tousled hair and growth of beard only increased Rick's sensual appeal. Suddenly frightened of her own desire, she backed away from him and tripped over a dining chair, sending herself sprawling and the chair clattering across the floor. The cat mewed at the window, scratching the screen with its claws and setting up an awful racket.

"I don't believe this," Rick muttered as he threw back the sheet and climbed off the daybed. "I'm stuck in this cabin with a nightwalker and a damn cat serenading me at the window." Unceremoniously he hauled Amy off the floor and banged on the window. The cat mewed several more times but, sensing that Rick was not going to feed her anymore, slipped away into the night. Amy was relieved to note that Rick was not naked, although the tight briefs he wore left little to the imagination. She murmured an apology and headed for the bedroom.

"Where are you going?" Rick growled as he picked up the dining chair.

"To bed," said Amy shortly.

"Don't be ridiculous!" Rick snapped as he returned to his daybed. "You'll suffocate in there. Get over there and go back to sleep!" he snarled as he pointed to her daybed.

"I can't do that," Amy protested.

"Why not?" Rick challenged gruffly.

"Because you're sleeping in here," Amy pointed out reasonably.

"So I am," Rick returned. "And if you think I'm going to be chivalrous and swelter in one of those bedrooms just to protect your Victorian notions of what's proper, you have another think coming. Besides, I've seen what you have to offer tonight, and I'm not tempted."

Unreasonably hurt, Amy stifled a sob and walked with dignity into the kitchen. With trembling fingers she poured a glass of milk and drank it quickly. She rinsed the glass and put it in the sink, then returned to the main room, noting that Rick had already returned to his daybed. Her eyes blurred by tears, she crawled into her daybed and turned her back to Rick. She did not hear him walk across the floor, but she felt the daybed sag and then felt gentle hands turn her over. He stared into her tear-stained face and wiped the moisture from her cheeks.

"I didn't mean that like it came out," Rick said softly. "For heaven's sake, don't go feeling unattractive now. I just meant that I'm tired, and I have no desire to take advantage of you, or any other woman, tonight. You're in no danger from me, and I want you to stay in here, where it's cool, otherwise you're going to be too hot to sleep." He reached down and lightly touched Amy's lips with his own.

The kiss began as a soft, comforting caress, but the inevitable fire burned between them again, and Amy felt herself clutching mindlessly to Rick, reveling in the feel of his soft lips on hers, quivering as his beard rasped her tender cheeks. He put one broad palm on either side of her head and held it immobile while he explored her mouth with his, running his tongue lightly around her lips and gasping when Amy returned his caress with a similar one of her own. She gave in to the temptation that she had fought all day and ran her fingers through the curling hair on his chest, luxuriating in the exciting sensations in her palms that the feel of his crisp hair and his hard chest created for her. Slowly she leaned back on the bed, drawing Rick with her until his body covered hers, his large warm frame comfortably heavy on her small one. She squirmed as she tried to fit her body just a little closer to his, and gasped in delight when she felt the evidence of Rick's growing desire for her. She locked her arms around his waist and pulled him closer to her, filling her nostrils with the heady scent of his clean, slightly sweaty body. This lovely sharing could not be carried to its natural conclusion and both of them knew it, but it was as if each of them wanted to savor as much of the warmth and sharing as they could before they called a halt. Rick reached down and caressed one small breast, tracing the hardened nipple with his finger through the thin cotton nightgown. He started to pull the gown down off her shoulders, then, with what seemed to be a mighty act of will, stopped his hand from baring her body to his. Amy felt the rush of cool air between their heated bodies and felt a disappointing loss.

Rick lifted his head and studied her with slumberous eyes. "If I keep holding you, I'm going to make love to you tonight, and neither of us really wants that right now. Now, you get some sleep."

Amy nodded wordlessly as Rick pulled away. Now, more than ever, she doubted the wisdom of sleeping in the same room as Rick, but admitted to herself that the bedrooms were stifling and that she would get no sleep in one of them. She watched Rick as he walked across the room and returned to his own bed, snapping out his light and staring out into the moonlit waters. In the white moonlight his body had the sheen of a pagan god come to life. Amy sucked in her breath at the fresh wave of desire that unraveled in her stomach. He would be the perfect lover. But he already had two women and did not need any more. Sighing, Amy turned over and slept, dreaming of gentle fingers wiping tears from her face, and a warm heavy body covering hers.

Amy woke to the sound of running water in the shower. She looked around the room, wondering if she, in fact, had only dreamed the events of the night before. They had an unreal quality about them, but the shorts and shirt wadded on the floor and the empty bowl on the front step convinced Amy that she had not been dreaming and that Rick really had dried the tears from her face and kissed her passionately before going back to his own bed. Turning over on her stomach and burying her head in the pillow, Amy wondered what on earth to do about the growing attraction she felt for Rick. If she was to keep working with him, she would have to curb that attraction somehow, and expose fewer of her emotions to him. Sighing into the pillow, she was snuggling further down under the sheet when a broad palm smacked her bottom soundly. Amy kicked out blindly, coming in contact with a bony knee.

"Hell, you're more dangerous in the morning than you are at night!" Rick grinned as he stripped the cozy sheet from her body. "Get up, woman, you have work to do today."

"I don't want to get up," Amy grumbled as she hugged the pillow against her.

"Uh-oh," Rick sighed. "A reluctant riser. Well, I know a cure for that one." Bending over, he grasped Amy's shoulders and pulled her firmly up. Before she could protest, his mouth swooped down and captured hers in a hard sweet kiss. One hand snaked around her slender waist and the other covered one small breast. Amy came awake with a start. Her lips returned his kiss with a flaming passion of their own. Rick bore her down on the bed, pressing her breasts into his firm chest, and explored her neck and shoulders with his mouth, creating a slow, warm liquid fire within her. Amy moaned in delight, protesting gently when he removed his lips from her shoulder and sat up. "Do we continue, or would you like to get up now?" he inquired wickedly.

"I'll get up," Amy said as she shot out of the bed, her face burning. Rick's laughter followed her to the bathroom until she banged the door behind her. What was going to happen now? She and Rick couldn't be together for five minutes without falling all over each other! She knew what it was on her part, she thought as she stared at her startled face in the mirror. Physical and emotional attraction unlike that she had ever known. Why didn't she feel this way with David, the man she supposedly loved? And what about Rick? What was it for him? Was it because he was sincerely attracted to her, or did he behave like that with every woman? Was it mutual, or was it convenience?

Disturbed by her confused thoughts, Amy washed and dressed quickly, returning to a huge breakfast of eggs, sausage, and toast. "You remembered," Amy said approvingly as she dove into her food.

"I was afraid you would eat the table legs if I didn't feed you enough," Rick said solemnly, his eyes dancing with laughter.

"Table legs aren't bad if you season them properly," Amy retorted demurely as she helped herself to another sausage.

The friendly sparring at the breakfast table set the tone for the day. They visited Lake LBJ again, finding the lake blessedly free of yesterday's traffic, and examined several more of the principal mussel beds of Amy's study. As they worked together in lively harmony Amy thought how pleasant it was to have a companion to work with her in the water. She had managed just fine after David had stopped coming, and would again when Rick's job was completed, but for now it was nice to have someone to talk to, to hand things to her, to label her bottles while she collected more samples, and to help her get the boat in and out of the water. Rick went beyond his professional role as photographer and served as an assistant to Amy, and she deeply appreciated his help. As he unhitched the trailer at the end of a long day, she laid her hand on his arm and squeezed it gently. He stopped his work and turned to face her, a quizzical smile on his face.

"I just wanted to thank you for all the help," Amy said shyly. "I got a lot more done than I usually do, and it was nice to have someone to talk to."

"I enjoyed it," Rick said sincerely. "It was a privilege that happened to fall my way, and I'm glad it did." He turned back to the boat, and Amy returned to the cabin to pack. A privilege? That was certainly a gracious way for Rick to feel about helping Dr. Thompson, Amy thought as she stuffed her dirty clothes back into her suitcase. For once the brilliant woman completely missed the point.

CHAPTER FIVE

"Let's talk about getting married," David said as he wiped his mouth and set his napkin aside. Amy nodded wordlessly. She had suspected from the expensive restaurant that David was treating her to that he planned to propose to her tonight. As the waiter cleared the table Amy gazed out the window at the tourists on the Riverwalk. David had chosen a romantic spot for his proposal, but his words and attitude were more those of a brother asking his sister to go to the movies than a man asking his love to marry him. Involuntarily she thought of Rick and the way he would propose to the woman that he loved. She wasn't sure just how Rick would go about it, but she was sure that it wouldn't be like this!

Aggravated with herself for even thinking of Rick at a time like this, Amy dragged her attention back to David and smiled at him. "All right, let's talk about getting married," she said.

David took a sip of water. "I think we could have a good life together," he said slowly. "We're in the same field and would have a lot of common ground there. We'll keep teaching, and in a year or two we'll start a family. Yes, we will have brilliant children." David smiled at the thought of heirs. "What do you say, Amy? Marry me?"

He forgot to tell me he loves me, Amy thought in dismay. Aloud she said, "I love you too, David, and would be delighted to become your wife."

David colored. "Of course I love you, Amy," he said gently. "That goes without saying. But you will marry me?"

"Of course," Amy said, somewhat mollified.

"Super!" David said. "Let's set the date for the fall, after you finish your book and we are a few weeks into the fall semester. Quick and simple. University chapel. No fuss."

Involuntarily Amy thought of the beautiful wedding that she had been to with Rick. She stifled her disappointment and nodded her head. "No fuss. But I will wear a white dress."

David nodded. "And flowers, of course. One attendant each. Your sister, my brother?" Amy nodded again. "Then that's what we'll do." David smiled happily as he left a tip on the table and rose abruptly.

He led Amy down the winding steps to the Riverwalk. The night was hot and humid, and Amy's hair curled in damp tendrils around her face. David took her hand and together they strolled along the wide sidewalk that followed the river. When they reached the ivy-covered wall under the bridge, David drew her into the shadows and took Amy into his arms. He kissed her firmly and deeply, and she returned his kiss eagerly and hoped in vain that the passion she and Rick had experienced would have magically transferred itself to David's embrace. Of course, it had not. Kissing David had been the mildly pleasurable event that it always was, but the bone-melting heat of Rick's embrace just was not there. What was she thinking of? She should not have even been thinking of Rick at a time like this! But she could not forget the piercing heat of his embraces, and his promise that he would kiss her often, every time she needed it. What would become of Rick's promise now? Would David's tepid kisses be enough to satisfy her, now that she had known so much more with Rick? Her cheeks burned as she acknowledged the fact that it would be very hard to forget Rick's embraces and be satisfied with David's. Flustered, she put her palms on David's shoulders and pushed him away gently.

David mistakenly attributed her red cheeks and shaken expression to excitement. "It's great, isn't it?" he asked as he took her hand. Belatedly Amy realized that David had drawn her under the same bridge where Rick had kissed her. Briefly Amy felt disloyal to Rick and then chided herself for doing so. Why should she feel disloyal to him? He had only been playing with her, while David had done her the honor of asking her to marry him.

She forced herself to smile at David. "Yes, it's great," she said, and she told herself that it really was.

The news of Amy's engagement was met with enthusiasm at Patterson's Pics. Betty Jean asked a dozen questions about David and their plans, and Joe kissed her cheek and subjected her to an afternoon of wedding night jokes. Only Rick greeted her news without comment. His lips thinned and his habitual mocking grin faded, but he said nothing as he walked into the black-and-white darkroom and slammed the door shut behind him. Betty Jean caught Amy's eye and shrugged her shoulders, looking toward the shuddering door in puzzlement. Amy returned the shrug, not willing to admit to Betty Jean that Rick did not approve of her plans to marry David. Amy was disappointed that Rick was so obviously disapproving of her plans. For some reason his approval would mean so much to her, a fact she hated to admit.

Dr. Thompson's reaction to Amy's news was just as disappointing. "Are you sure, girl?" he asked as he leaned back in his chair and peered at her over the desk. "Are you very sure?"

Amy's gaze wandered around the cluttered, homey office and out the window to the peaceful campus, sleepy in the summer heat. She realized that she loved this school and this kindly gentleman for whom she worked. Looking at Dr. Thompson, she realized just how important his approval was to her. "Why shouldn't I be sure?" she asked quietly.

"I don't know, but something tells me you're not," the astute gentleman replied.

"I guess—I'm sure," Amy stammered. "We—David and I—we have a lot in common, our research and our teaching and everything. And we could have a good life together and a family." And he's the only one who wants me, she added to herself.

"How about your emotions, Amy? Does it set you on fire when David takes you into his arms?"

"Dr. Thompson!" Amy protested quietly.

"No, don't answer that." He laughed. "But seriously, Amy, the spark has to be there if you and David are going to have the kind of marriage that you deserve. If that fire is present, then forget that this meddling old man said anything. But if it isn't, think twice about what you're planning to do. Take it from me, Amy. As my love and I knew, that little spark makes all the difference."

Dr. Thompson's words echoed in Amy's head for the better part of the day. As she cataloged piles of mussel shells in the deserted laboratory, she thought about what he had said. He spoke of fire, of sparks, yet, if his relationship with his wife was anything to go by, Dr. Thompson's marriage had not been the exciting union he prescribed for Amy. His advice did make good sense, and Amy feared that she and David would never know that exquisite ecstasy. But what other alternative is there for me? she asked herself as she threw a particularly large mussel shell into the proper drawer. David, or another man like him, is the only kind of man that I don't scare to death. Unwittingly Rick's mocking face floated across Amy's mind. Somehow she did not seem to scare him!

"I need you to go on a job with me," Rick said to Amy as he unloaded his camera bag onto the work table. Amy was becoming very used to those words coming from Rick or one of the other photographers. In the three weeks she had been working at Patterson's Pics, she had made herself very useful as a gofer on complicated location jobs, and nearly every day one of the photographers took her on a job to assist. Amy was becoming very good at handling lights and changing film, and she enjoyed the endless variety of people she met and places she went. One day Tommy Lee had taken her to the one of the local breweries, and they had taken pictures of the entire process of brewing thousands of gallons of beer at once, at one point narrowly escaping when a vat of bubbling beer overflowed, pouring hundreds of gallons of hot foaming froth all over the brewery floor. Another day she and Rick followed San Antonio's energetic young mayor on a walk through downtown, photographing the talented politician as he talked with his constituents.

Amy thrived on the interesting change that working for Rick Patterson had brought to her life. Amazingly, even as her status as a college professor and researcher became known at the office, these people seemed to think of her as just another person, and Amy loved it. She suspected that Rick's casual acceptance of her as just another human being had a lot to do with the attitude of the others. If he thought of her as one of the gang, then why shouldn't they?

"Amy, did you hear me?" Rick asked impatiently. "I said we had a job to go to."

Amy snapped out of her reverie. "Sure," she said quickly. "Where to today?"

"I'm doing Samantha Westermann's stills for her new TV commercial. Remember Samantha? I think you met her once."

Yes, I met the poor woman, thought Amy to herself. Aloud she said yes, that she had met Samantha on the first day she had worked for him. Amy had not seen Samantha since she had met her and realized that Rick was two-timing her. Knowing what she did, she dreaded the thought of meeting the woman face to face again. But short of a miracle, there was no way the meeting could be avoided.

Amy sat in silence on the way to Samantha's boutique. Rick looked at her quizzically but did not try to force a conversation. Since she had announced her engagement, he had been courteous to her, but the teasing intimacy they had shared on the first trip to the lakes was gone. They had made one more trip to the lakes since the first, but Rick was so cool and distant, Amy may as well have been with a different man. He had made no move to kiss her, despite his promise that he would kiss her often, and Amy was a little disappointed that he had not done so. He seemed vaguely contemptuous of her at times, although at others she was convinced that the contempt was all in her imagination. He had not mentioned her engagement to David and neither had she.

Amy's dread of the meeting with Samantha proved unfounded. Amy was able to act completely natural when the older woman greeted Amy cordially and hugged Rick with enthusiasm. In spite of herself, Amy felt a quick thrust of jealousy at the warmth of their exchange. While Rick and Samantha discussed with the models exactly what pictures Samantha needed, Amy wandered around the delightful little boutique. Samantha had designed the shop to cater to the young career woman with more taste and ambition than money, and her buyers had gathered together a delightful selection of daywear and dresses at reasonable prices, although there was also a selection of more expensive clothing for the successful woman who could afford them. Samantha's boutique filled a needed niche and with proper advertising would continue to do a brisk business. Amy browsed the rack of dresses in her size and found several that she would love to own, and she promised herself that she would come back another day and try on the dresses.

As she wandered back to Rick and Samantha she became aware that the models had gone to change and that Rick had begun setting up without her. "Sorry," she mumbled as she unfolded a tripod.

"That's all right," Samantha said. "I told Rick not to call you

92

until you had chosen at least two dresses. Did you see anything you like?"

"Samantha!" Rick chided. "Watch it, Amy. This woman's a born salesperson. She will sell you half the store if you're not careful." Rick smiled at Samantha indulgently.

"I found two that I really like, but they will have to wait until later, when I have time to try them on," Amy replied. "Maybe I'll buy them for my trousseau."

"You're getting married?" Samantha asked. "Congratulations. When is the big day?"

"Sometime in the fall," Amy said. "After my book is finished and we're into the fall semester."

"Well, best wishes. I've never been married myself, have no desire to, actually, but I wish the best for you if that's what you want," Samantha said as she stepped back to make room for Rick to set up his first shot.

Rick and Amy worked for the better part of the afternoon shooting Samantha's advertising stills. Between Rick and Samantha they had come up with what was surely one of the most effective advertising ideas that Amy had ever seen. Instead of draping a dress over a chair or hiring beautiful models, Rick had deliberately hired women who looked like the typical working woman. Some were young, some were not so young, some were prettier than others, but all had that tired-after-a-hard-day-at-the-office look that most career woman had earned by five in the afternoon. He then photographed them browsing in the boutique, pulling clothes off the rack and holding them up in the mirror, trying them on, and purchasing them with their own check or credit card. The models, most of whom had just spent the better part of the day actually working in an office, got into the spirit of the job, and Rick successfully captured the delight felt by a woman selecting pretty clothing that suited her life-style and her pocketbook.

Pleased at the results of the afternoon's efforts, Samantha invited Rick and Amy to share supper with her at her apartment.

Amy started to decline, but Rick accepted for the two of them, and since Amy was without transportation, it was pointless for her to refuse. Besides, she was curious about Samantha's home.

Rick followed Samantha's bright blue Porsche the few blocks to Samantha's apartment, located in an expensive highrise. Rick parked his van and took the elevator up to the eighth floor with the ease of a familiar visitor. He took the key from Samantha and inserted it in the lock, and Samantha smiled indulgently at the proprietary gesture. Amy gulped in awe at Samantha's luxurious furnishings and the valuable art that covered the walls, comparing them to her own primitive oak antiques and simple watercolors. Samantha's housekeeper, a middle-aged Mexican woman, clucked over the new dress that Samantha had brought for her, and quickly tried it on, thanking Samantha profusely in a stream of Spanish. Samantha thanked the housekeeper for having such a delicious meal prepared, but shooed the woman home and set the table and made the coffee herself.

Rick perched on a counter stool while he and Samantha chattered comfortably about mutual friends and concerns, and Amy listened with half her mind, using the other half to speculate on the curious relationship between Rick and Samantha. Their manner seemed warm and intimate but not particularly sensual, and he was sleeping with another woman. Was their love life less than satisfactory to Rick? Had they been lovers too long? Or was Rick just a born philanderer? If she had not become engaged to David, would Rick have continued his pursuit of her?

"I noticed that you were looking through my size five rack, Amy," Samantha said as Rick seated them both at the table. He sat down between them, facing neither.

Amy nodded. "That's the size I wear," she said ruefully. "Frankly, I'd give anything to be a little bigger."

"Why?" Samantha asked in astonishment. "I would love to be your size."

"You look wonderful, Samantha," Rick said fondly. "I wouldn't want you any other way." A sharp stab of jealousy knifed through Amy's midsection. Had Rick only been flattering her that day on the boat?

"No, Amy, I wasn't just flattering you the other day," Rick said smoothly. Amy choked on a mouthful of the delicious chicken she was eating. The man was a mind reader! Turning to Samantha, Rick said, "Amy doesn't think she is attractive."

"That's ridiculous," Samantha said. "Of course you're attractive. But I have the feeling there's something else behind your wish to be larger. Something practical."

"There is," Amy admitted. "I'm so thin that there is not much of a selection of sophisticated clothing in my size. Everything that fits me has a bow in the back, which was fine when I was in high school, but it's getting to be a pain now. You have more than anyone else, but the rack is still smaller than all the others."

Samantha gazed thoughtfully at Amy for a moment, then her face lit up and she turned to Rick excitedly. "That's it! I've been thinking about opening another specialty store next door. Amy has given me an idea. There are bound to be other women like her out there, old enough to wear sophisticated clothes but too small to find them! The store could carry size five and under for the over-twenty-five crowd. Would you patronize a shop like that, Amy?"

"Heavens, yes," Amy replied. "Would you really open a shop like that?"

"Sounds good to me, Samantha," Rick said warmly. "If you'll do it, I'll help you get it off the ground."

"Thank you, Rick. I can always count on you," Samantha said with love in her eyes. The look of warmth and love that Rick returned to Samantha made Amy turn away involuntarily. Why couldn't Rick look at her like that? Amy admitted to herself that it was not reasonable to want that kind of affection from him, but she craved it in spite of herself.

"I'll get started right away, now that I have the idea," Samantha said musingly.

Rick and Amy left soon after they had finished their coffee, all three of them admitting to fatigue and the long day behind them. Samantha did look tired, but it did not detract from her vibrant beauty. As they prepared to leave the apartment, Rick took Samantha into his arms and tipped her face up to his. "Take care of yourself," he admonished quietly as he kissed her on the cheek and held her close. "I'll see you in a few days."

Samantha nodded wordlessly. Amy felt bewildered and sad, and was not really sure why. But Amy was sure of one thing. Whatever his behavior with Linda or any other woman, Rick Patterson loved Samantha Westermann. He loved her very much.

"Do you like it, Amy?" David asked eagerly as he placed the gaudy ring on her finger.

Amy nodded wordlessly as she stared down at the elaborate diamond and sapphire cluster on her hand. She couldn't very well say that she did not like it, but, in fact, she didn't. Amy had always preferred plain, simple jewelry, something that would not overpower her tiny features. This ring was too large for her thin fingers and made her look and feel like a little girl playing in her mother's jewelry box. However, since David had obviously chosen the ring himself and gone into debt for it, she felt that she had no choice but to accept and wear the ring graciously and later choose a simple wedding band that she could wear alone, saving this one for special occasions. "It's—beautiful," she stammered. "I'll always treasure it."

"I thought you would," David said as he picked up her hand and admired the ring. "It's really very feminine," he said.

I wonder if I can change his taste later, Amy thought as they drove to a movie. Probably no more than he could change mine, she admitted to herself. Not that David's taste was bad; it was just so different from her own. David sat preoccupied through the movie, even though it had been one of his own choosing, and Amy sensed that something was troubling him. She knew that if she waited long enough, David would tell her what was on his mind. And he did, over hamburgers and beer after the movie.

"Have you heard anything about the associate position?" David shouted over the noisy din in the restaurant.

"No," Amy shouted back. At that moment some obliging soul turned down the sound system so that, while still noisy, the restaurant was quiet enough so that the patrons could carry on an intelligent conversation. Lowering her voice, she continued. "They're later than usual announcing promotions this year, but I haven't heard a word about who the lucky people are going to be. Why? Getting antsy?"

"Yes," David admitted, coloring. "I think I have a good chance for that position. In fact, I just have to get it."

"And why do you just 'have' to get it?" Amy asked teasingly.

David looked at her sheepishly. "Let's just say that I want it an awful lot. I need the prestige being an associate would give me," he added. "My book will be good, but the competition out there is fierce."

"We both knew that when we went after this kind of life," Amy said quietly. "And your book is better than good. On the basis of that alone you could get a job or a promotion most anywhere there is an opening." David shrugged noncommitally and Amy's irritation flared. "What do you want me to do, hold your hand and tell you that you're the best? You are and you know it, so stop whining to me." She tapped the table impatiently with her forefinger.

David grinned ruefully. "You're probably right. Depend on good old Amy to give a fellow a kick in the pants when he needs it! Sorry I aggravated you." He looked at his watch and groaned. "It's late and I've got to teach that damn seven A.M. class. Let's go, Amy." He looked down and caught Amy's left hand in his, then tipped up the ring and let the light from the ceiling catch in the stones and send a rainbow onto the wall. "I knew you would like it!"

* * *

Amy kept her promise to Samantha and dropped by the boutique one morning after a class to try on the dresses she had liked. Samantha and both of her salesgirls were busy with other customers, so Amy found the dresses and made her way to the fitting rooms. One of the dresses was not as attractive on Amy as it had been on the hanger, but the other was perfect for work or business. It was a superbly cut wheat-colored linen wrap dress with a stand-up collar and a belt in navy blue, the excellent cut emphasizing Amy's tiny waist. With simple gold jewelry it would be perfect.

Amy browsed for a few more minutes but saw nothing else that interested her, so she made her way to the cash register and fished out her checkbook from the depths of her purse. The other salesgirls were still busy, but Samantha's customer had left and Samantha was completing the transaction on the cash register. Looking up, she spotted Amy and smiled warmly. "I see you did come back for the dress," she said.

Amy nodded. "The blue one didn't look so good on, but this one is just what I need," she replied.

Samantha agreed. "I buy a lot from this designer for that very reason. He designs for the career woman."

"Do you wear his clothes yourself?" Amy asked, sneaking a look at the label.

"Yes, I wear his clothes often," Samantha replied. They chatted amiably while Samantha rang up the sale, then Samantha handed Amy her sack with a warm, sincere smile. "I really enjoyed seeing you again the other day. Rick has said so many nice things about you and your work. He must think the world of you."

"I'm sure that he thinks the world of you, too," Amy returned, thinking that would please Samantha.

Surprisingly Samantha shook her head. "Sometimes I wish he didn't think so much of me," she said quietly.

Amy speculated on Samantha's peculiar statement on and off for the rest of the day. Rather than seeming concerned because

Rick thought too little of her, Samantha seemed concerned that Rick thought too much. Amy had quite a bit of faith in her ability to judge what people were like, and she felt sure that Samantha would be the last woman who would want or tolerate an open relationship, so there had to be another explanation for her cryptic comment. Amy speculated on the mystery that night while she graded a stack of papers, but no solution was forthcoming.

CHAPTER SIX

Amy reached over and slapped at the alarm, and then realized that the unwelcome interruption into her slumber was the ringing telephone. Uttering a muffled curse, she snapped on the bedside lamp and fumbled for the receiver. "Yes, Mother, what is it?" She yawned into the mouthpiece.

"Well, that's a more civil response than I expected at this hour," a friendly voice rumbled in her ear. "Mama calls you early?"

Confused, Amy sat up and blinked rapidly. "Why are you calling me so early, Rick?" she demanded.

"Now, you can be just as nice to me as you would have been to your mother!" he said in a teasing voice. Amy knew he was grinning. "I have a big favor to ask, pretty lady."

It's been a long time since he's called me that, Amy thought. Aloud she said, "And what can I do for you at six fifteen in the morning?"

"I can think of several things, some more fun than others," he replied wickedly. "But what I really need is for you to go with me on an out-of-town assignment today. Tommy Lee's too sick to go, and I need help."

100

"I have to teach this morning," Amy said firmly.

"Look, I know it's a lot to ask, but I need you badly," Rick wheedled. He was at his most charming, and Amy was weakening. "Couldn't David take your class for you this once?"

"I'll ask him. Call me back in five minutes," Amy capitulated. "Oh, hell," she muttered as she stabbed at the buttons on her phone in irritation. He could have given her some warning yesterday.

David answered sleepily and with a little persuasion agreed to teach the class. She hung up the telephone and laid back on the pillow, realizing that she had no idea where they were going or how she should dress. She shut her eyes and jumped when the telephone rang for the second time.

"Bet I woke you back up," Rick said smoothly. "We're shooting an advertising layout for a west Texas resort. I'll pick you up in twenty minutes."

Amy banged the telephone in his ear. Twenty minutes! The man was a monster!

Exactly twenty-one minutes later the doorbell rang. Amy was dressed in jeans and a smock but she had not yet put on her makeup or consumed a cup of coffee. Rick paced while she swiftly applied lipstick and mascara, and she grudgingly skipped her coffee. He hustled her out to his van and opened the driver's door. She squeezed in and scooted over, and gratefully accepted an apple from him. "There's coffee in a thermos if you want it, pretty lady," he added.

"Thanks, Rick," she replied gratefully. She munched on the apple and stared out of the windshield as Rick drove through the light early morning traffic and took the highway that would lead them to the resort. Amy's trained eye watched the changing landscape with interest. An ecologist could see four distinct ecosystems by driving just a few miles outside of San Antonio in each of the four directions. To the north he would find the Hill Country. To the east he would find rolling black farmland and the trees and flowers of east Texas. To the south and southeast

101

he would find grassy coastal plains, and to the west he would see, as Amy was now seeing, rough, rocky land interspersed with mesquite trees and shrubs. This land was not as beautiful to her as her beloved Hill Country, but it was striking in a desolate way, and she observed it keenly.

Rick passed Amy a small thermos of coffee, and to avoid a spill she drank straight from the thermos, refusing a styrofoam cup. He extended his hand and, wordlessly, Amy handed him the thermos. He drank from it also, deliberately placing his mouth directly over Amy's lipstick stain, then handed the thermos back to her. She took another swallow of the scalding liquid, and together they finished the coffee, first one and then the other sipping the strong brew. Then, in a boldly intimate gesture, Amy reached up and wiped a drop of coffee off Rick's upper lip. His lips playfully closed over her finger and he nibbled it lightly. Amy withdrew her finger and returned the thermos to the hamper on the floor. She sat quietly, savoring the intimate exchange with Rick and, without meaning to, remembering the kisses they had shared all too long ago.

Fort Wilson was an abandoned army fort that had been left to decay for a number of years before a national development company purchased the property. Ed Golden, the slick middle-aged representative of the company, proudly told them that the developers had spent two years and several million dollars renovating the old fort, and Amy had to admit that the results were impressive. The officers' homes had been remodeled and sold to private individuals to use as a weekend retreat or a retirement home, and the barracks had been reconstructed as tasteful lodges. The mess hall was now an inexpensive cafeteria, and swimming pools, tennis courts, and a stable had been added. Ed explained that the developers planned to add more amenities in the future, when the resort was making a profit.

Amy gazed across the grounds appreciatively. There were large oak trees lining the gravel streets, and lush grass underfoot, in direct contrast to the harsh landscape outside the fort. She suspected that the original fort had been built over an underground water supply. In addition, a recent rain had left puddles in the streets and made the ground springy to walk on. Amy absently swatted a mosquito off her neck and followed Ed Golden and Rick to the stable, where they were to take the first photographs. Rick mentioned casually that he intended to climb the rickety water tower later in the day to make some shots from the top, and Amy stared up at the spindly platform and tried not to wince.

The family coming in from their morning ride were more than glad to serve as models. Rick explained that it would cost an exorbitant amount of money to hire enough professional models to come all the way to Fort Wilson and pose all day, and that Ed had decided to use the actual guests as models. The accommodating family posed saddling their mounts, riding down a marked trail, and the mother, an excellent horsewoman, agreed to be photographed racing her horse across an open field and jumping it over a low fence. Rick captured the woman in the middle of the leap, long blond hair loose and flying, horse and woman in perfect harmony. Amy knew that shot would make the brochure.

They spent most of the morning trailing around after Ed, lighting and shooting interiors and waiting for the clouds to clear. Amy enjoyed seeing the luxurious private homes and meeting the mostly elderly couples that inhabited them. Amy supposed that there would be more young people around on the weekends. Ed fed them a tasty lunch after they had photographed the cafeteria, and Rick stifled his laughter at the look on Ed's face when Amy went back to the buffet table for her third helping of fried chicken.

The clouds had cleared by the time they had finished lunch, and Rick decided to try the water tower shot. Amy cringed as Rick climbed up the spindly ladder, but he made it to the top with the effortless grace of a teenager. He spent long minutes on the platform while Amy craned her neck and watched him, squinting into the sun until her eyes watered and swatting at mosquitos on her arms. Rick took pictures in every direction and then tumbled down the ladder with the agility of a monkey. When Rick's feet hit the ground, Amy expelled a sigh of relief.

"I want you to take something with a pretty girl in it," Ed said to Rick as they walked toward the tennis courts. "Every brochure needs at least one cheesecake shot." Ed slapped at a mosquito that was making a meal of his neck.

"Fine," Rick said. "Where? Tennis court or swimming pool?"

"Either one," Ed replied. "I'm not picky."

They went first to the tennis courts, where they photographed a middle-aged couple fiercely competing for a wagered drink. Then they went to the swimming pool, a spring-fed olympic pool surrounded by oak trees. Rick took pictures of a few children playing at one end of the pool and a young teenaged boy diving from the high board. Ed looked around anxiously. "I just don't see any young girls around. Damn, and I was counting on at least one cheesecake!"

"I see one," Rick said thoughtfully, looking Amy up and down. "We're changing your assignment today, Amy." Rick laughed. "You get to be our cheesecake."

"Me? You have to be kidding!" Amy said in amusement, although deep inside her a tiny hope blossomed. One of her girlhood fantasies had been to be a glamorous fashion model, complete with carefully windblown hair and seductive smile. And now she might get the chance to live out that fantasy.

Ed Golden caught Rick's eye and shook his head. "I was thinking of someone a little more, well, uh—"

"He means that I'm too flat," Amy said dryly. "And he's right. Cheesecake needs bosom."

"Nonsense," Rick said briskly. "She looks great. Isn't your daughter about her size? Some of her things ought to fit."

Ed still looked doubtful. "Well, if you say so," he said reluctantly. "My daughter left some of her things in my apartment.

I'll take you over there and you can change. Rick, do you want her to pose on the tennis courts or in the pool?"

"Both," Rick said absently as he swatted a mosquito on his arm.

Ed's daughter was just Amy's size, and in the closet Amy found both a suitable tennis dress and a daringly cut maillot. She donned the tennis dress first and borrowed some of the girl's cosmetics and made up her face the way she had seen the models do theirs for shooting sessions. Grabbing a tennis racket, she returned to the tennis courts and waited while Rick set up a tripod. Rick motioned her out on to the court and told her to hit a few balls.

Belatedly Amy realized that she did not know the first thing about playing tennis. How would she ever hit the ball in a halfway realistic manner? She wiped her sweaty palms on her bare legs, swatted away a persistent mosquito, and valiantly picked up a tennis ball. Throwing it up over her head, she swiped at the falling ball and missed it, smacking herself in the leg instead. Too embarrassed to look over at the men, she picked up another ball and swatted at it, this time hitting it to one side and causing a couple of interested spectators to dodge. She sneaked a look in Rick's direction, afraid he might be angry, and instead felt herself become infuriated by his wicked grin. She gripped the racket so hard that her nails bit into her palms and tossed another ball into the air, hitting it smartly with the racket. This one flew through the air perfectly, landing in the opposite court and bouncing firmly. She looked over at Rick excitedly. "Did you get that shot?" she asked triumphantly.

"Yes, I got it," Rick said as he walked over to her and removed the tennis racket from her hand. "But I won't be able to use it. You weren't smiling!"

Amy uttered a very unladylike word.

Ed rushed toward them, shaking his head. "That isn't what I'm looking for at all," he frowned. "We have action shots already. I want a closeup of her in something sexy. I want the ads to appeal to something other than Mom's desire to relax and play tennis."

"You want to appeal to all those lustful daddies out there who will bring Mom and the kids here," Rick joked.

Amy motioned Rick aside. "I can't do that kind of thing, Rick," she whispered. "I just don't look that good!"

"For God's sake, don't go all shy on me now," he whispered back in irritation. "If you won't do it, I'll have to bring Stella back one day next week, and it will shoot another day and most of my profits on the job. You have to do this." His irritation faded and his familiar grin appeared. "And, yes, you do look that good."

For Rick's sake, she forced herself to nod her head. "You've got yourself a sex goddess," she said firmly.

She returned to Ed's apartment and donned the sexy swimsuit she had found earlier. It was bright coral and was daringly cut out in a curving pattern under her breasts and below her waist, exposing large patches of Amy's supple tanned skin. Although it covered more of her than her usual bikini, the effect was certainly more sensuous, and Amy almost felt that she could be the sexy siren that Ed wanted. She repaired her makeup and sauntered out to the pool, where Ed broke off his conversation to whistle at her and slap at a hungry mosquito. "My apologies, Amy. You look divine!"

Rick was unsurprised. "I knew she would look great," he said calmly. "I've seen her without her clothes before." Ignoring Amy's look of pure rage, he spread out a beach towel and motioned to Amy. "Spread out on that and look back at me," he ordered.

Amy lay down stiffly on the towel and turned around to Rick. He shook his head and came over to her. "Like this," he said, bending one of Amy's knees slightly and curving one arm over her thigh. "Now, stare right into the lens with a come-hither look in your eyes," he instructed her.

He snapped one picture and swore as Amy moved her arm to

slap at a mosquito. "You're going to have to hold still," he snapped irritably. "You can scratch later." Biting back a sarcastic remark, she resumed her pose.

Rick took three more pictures and stopped again. "You have about as much expression as a wooden Indian," he snarled. "Pretend you're about to make love to David! Now, come on!"

Valiantly Amy tried to imagine herself seducing David and failed. In David's place, Rick's face kept popping up. A bit out of curiosity, Amy let her fantasy move in that direction. She was smiling at Rick, inviting him into her bed. He was coming to her, kissing her, slipping the gown from her shoulders, carrying her into the bedroom, lying her on the bed . . .

"Amy! Sit up now! I want you to change poses." Amy sat up, her cheeks burning. If Rick had not broken into her reverie, she would have let her imagination go on to wherever and enjoyed every minute of it. She blinked as Rick came toward her and moved her body into a languorous sitting position. Although his touch was impersonal, after her vivid fantasy each touch on her flesh was like fire. She felt her nipples harden and hoped they did not show through the fabric of the suit. Rick muttered something under his breath that Amy did not quite catch, but she thought she heard "David" and "lucky bastard."

She and Rick worked by the pool for more than an hour. Rick posed her sitting by the pool, sprawled in abandon on the towel, seductively draped over the diving board, and dangling her feet in the water. Amy soon became tired of posing, particularly as she did not have the freedom to reach down and swat away the mosquitos that were feasting on her bare stomach and midriff, which were on fire from the stinging bites. The surface of the diving board scratched her back and sides, and she refused to complain, although her childhood fantasy of modeling was quickly being shattered by this experience. Modeling was hard work!

Finally Rick signaled that he was through. Gratefully Amy rolled off the diving board into the icy water and swam several laps, enjoying the feel of the cold water on her scratched back and numerous mosquito bites. Refreshed, she climbed out of the pool and joined the men, who were packing up the equipment and storing the exposed rolls of film in a separate pouch. Despite the fact that she was dripping wet, Ed put his arm around her and gave her a big hug. "You were great," he said warmly. "Maybe you should consider a career as a model."

"Oh, I don't think so." Rick laughed. "Amy's a professor at the university."

Ed thought for a moment, then withdrew his arm from Amy quickly, as though he thought it might embarrass her to be close to him. "Of course, you're Dr. Walsh. My daughter said you were one of the best profs she ever had. She said you were doing some real important research and all." Suddenly Ed's manner went from comfortable to awkward. "I'm sure sorry if we inconvenienced you with all this posing, Dr. Walsh—a professional lady like you."

"You didn't inconvenience me in the least, Ed," she said gently. "And, please—I'm just Amy."

But Ed never could quite relax around Amy for the rest of the day. He stammered and tried to use all the impressive words he knew. Over supper in the cafeteria, he asked her endless questions about her research, and she tried to answer them as simply as she could without talking down to him. Catching her eye, Rick smiled ruefully and, at the barely perceptible nod of her head, he broke in and changed the subject.

Crawling back into the van, Amy scratched the mosquito bites on her stomach through the smock and tried to ignore the itching and the welts on her legs and arms. As Rick sank into the seat beside her Amy realized that his nose was red. Amy, with her skin browned by hours at the lake, did not show the effects of the hot west Texas sun. She was tired, though, and allowed her body to relax into the seat. She realized that her hip and thigh were pressed close to Rick's, but she did not have the

108

energy to move away, and besides, the sensation was distinctly pleasant.

Rick took the highway that would lead them back to San Antonio. They sat comfortably, chatting idly about their shooting day, and Rick commented that he was sorry that Tommy Lee had not been able to come with him.

"Yes, I'm sure he would have been a lot more help than I was," Amy admitted ruefully.

"Absolutely not," Rick said firmly. "He couldn't have done a thing for that swimsuit. But I wanted him to get a little of that sort of experience."

Amy cocked her head to one side. "Just how old is Tommy Lee, anyway?" she asked curiously.

"Not quite nineteen," Rick replied. "He's been working for me for just over a year now. I hired him just out of high school."

"How did he get started taking pictures?" Amy asked.

"Same way I did. His mother gave him a camera when he was just little, and from then on that's all either of us ever wanted to do. He walked into the office one day out of the blue and asked for a job. I was about to show him the door when I decided to look at his portfolio, just out of courtesy. I hired him on the spot."

"How about college?" Amy asked.

"No point in that," Rick said. "I can teach him what he needs."

"It's a shame he didn't go to college," Amy said musingly. "At least for a year or two."

"Why?" Rick replied tersely. "He doesn't need it. I didn't."

"Sorry," Amy said. "I didn't realize that you hadn't been to school. Or have you?"

"Oh, yes, I have a business degree that hangs in my office and gathers dust. I use it once a year when I do my income tax," he replied.

Amy scratched her itching arms. "But won't he need something later?" she argued.

"Probably not," Rick said lightly. "What I failed to mention is that he is about the best photographer that I have ever worked with, without even allowing for his inexperience. In a couple of years some big New York or Los Angeles studio is going to lure him away from me. He will go farther than I ever will, and maybe even farther than you. So don't worry about him. He doesn't need college, so there's no point in his going."

"But everybody needs a college education," Amy said firmly.

"No, they don't," Rick said equally firmly. "If a person is going to do something with that education, fine. But if they aren't, why bother?"

They said no more, but Amy pondered Rick's practical view of higher education. Among Amy's colleagues, it was assumed that everyone needed to attend college and that the lack of at least one degree was a serious handicap to one's future. Amy had readily accepted this philosophy, thinking of her own success academically, yet she had to admit that Rick's point of view made sense. Why should someone like Tommy Lee spend four years learning something that he would never use, when he could be perfecting his talent with Rick?

Amy sat silently and watched the sun go down on the harsh landscape. She tried to ignore the itching mass of mosquito bites that her body was becoming, but with each passing mile, that became increasingly difficult. She squirmed in the seat and scratched at her arms and legs, rubbing her bitten back into the upholstery in a effort to relieve her misery. The stings on her stomach were particularly uncomfortable, but Amy could not scratch them because of the seat belt. Soon each mile was agony, but she said nothing to Rick and just hoped that he would drive fast and deliver her home so she could put something soothing on her miserable flesh. Rick looked over several times, but Amy managed to control her scratching until he returned his gaze to the road.

The moon shone brightly over the bleak landscape, throwing

a silvery sheen on the scrubby brush. In the distance Amy imagined that she saw the shining eyes of white-tailed deer, but in the moonlight she could not be sure. Under other circumstances she might have found the drive profoundly romantic, but in her itchy state she could not get back to San Antonio soon enough. She watched the horizon eagerly, and rejoiced when the first faint glow of the San Antonio skyline appeared.

By the time they had reached the city limits, Amy was aware that she was not experiencing just the usual irritating itching from mosquito bites. Her tongue felt thick, and she felt so agitated that she was almost ready to jump out of the van. She had nothing in her apartment for the kind of reaction she was having, and as much as she hated to bother him, she would be forced to ask Rick's assistance.

"Rick," she said slowly through thick lips.

Rick turned slightly to her, then jerked the van to the shoulder of the road and braked suddenly. He turned on the overhead light and swore softly, then lightly brushed Amy's face with his hand. It was hot and tight to his touch. He turned again to the wheel and roared down the highway, breaking every speed law in the state of Texas. "My God, woman, why didn't you say something sooner?" he snarled as he whipped around a cloverleaf and got on the expressway.

Amy reached up and touched her face. Her features were swollen and the skin was hot and taut. "Lord, I didn't realize it was doing this," she forced out.

"Don't talk anymore," Rick ordered. Amy was only too glad to obey. The agitation was getting worse, and it was all she could do to keep from screaming.

Rick drove to an unfamiliar subdivision and parked his car in front of a prosperous but not exorbitant row of town houses. He unlocked the front door and escorted Amy inside, sitting her down on the sofa and going straight to the telephone in the kitchen. Almost immediately he was dialing a number and then was back in the dining room, tangling his fingers in the telephone

111

cord and looking at Amy anxiously. Amy looked down at her blotchy and swollen fingers and sincerely hoped that Rick located a doctor very soon.

Finally Rick received a response on the other end. "Mom? This is Rick. Look, Amy Walsh and I were out on an assignment today, and she got eaten alive by mosquitos. Yes, hives and swollen tongue and joints. Should I take her to the emergency room? You think an oral medication will do? Just a moment." Rick turned to Amy. "Are you allergic to any antihistamine that you know of?"

"Just sulfa," she replied.

"Just sulfa. Can you telephone that to the pharmacy on the corner here? I don't want to leave her for too long. She's highly agitated, and I don't want her to chew a hole in my throw pillow." Rick ducked as Amy chucked the pillow at him.

Rick grabbed his checkbook and flew out the door, leaving Amy grinding her teeth in agitation, but not too miserable to be surprised. So Rick's mother was a doctor. She should have suspected something like that. The fact that Rick was not intimidated by her should have told her that he was used to being around a strong, bright woman. She wondered if his father was also a doctor and guessed that he was.

Before too many minutes had passed, Rick was back with a small vial filled with huge purple capsules. He shook two into her hand and got her a glass of water from the kitchen. Amy swallowed the pills with the water gratefully and sank back on the sofa, willing the itching and the agitation to go away. Idly she pulled up her blouse and gasped when she saw the angry red welts on her midriff, where the daring bathing suit had bared her skin to the mosquitos.

"They'll go away," Rick volunteered as he gently rubbed the inflamed skin with the palm of his hand. The gentle abrasion of his rough palm was curiously soothing to the sensitive skin, and Amy lay back and let Rick minister to her. He absently rubbed her midriff as he flipped through his mail, not stopping until he had examined the entire stack. His light, tender touch was both soothing and exciting.

"Feeling better?" he asked gently in a few minutes.

Amy nodded. The purple pills were having an almost miraculous effect on Amy's system, and before their eyes, the swelling went down and Amy's sharp features reappeared. The welts on her legs and arms were still visible, but not so pronounced as before. Rick grinned as he noted the changes.

"Mom said to tell you that she is looking forward to your new book," Rick volunteered. "She enjoyed the last one thoroughly."

"She's familiar with Dr. Thompson's work, then," Amy said.

"Oh, yes, they went to school together and dated for a while, and then Mom met Dad, and that was that. But Mom and Harold remained good friends."

"Is your father a doctor also?" Amy asked.

"Yes, he is, and so are both of my brothers," admitted Rick. "I'm the black sheep."

"Surely you don't mean that!" Amy scolded. "Why, any parent alive would be proud to have you for a son."

"Thanks," Rick said dryly. "They are, but they had always dreamed that all their children would be doctors, as they were," he replied with a twinkle in his eye. "And then here I came, with a girl under one arm and a camera under the other. They gave up on me after they saw my grades as a college freshman. After I graduated and got some experience with another studio, they helped me start Patterson's, so I don't think they're too disappointed in me."

"I should think not!" Amy exclaimed indignantly. She herself would be proud to mother a son like Rick. She examined her hands and midriff, then looked at the clock. "I feel a lot better and it's getting late. Why don't you run me on home now?"

"No," Rick said baldly.

"What?" Amy asked indignantly, jerking her head back.

"I said no," Rick said again. "You're still suffering from a

113

severe allergic reaction, and only in the last few minutes has it been under control. You shouldn't be alone."

"That's nonsense," Amy replied. Rick was being ridiculous in her opinion. She was fine. "I'm leaving." She sat up, but Rick pushed her back into the cushions and walked back to the telephone. He quickly dialed his mother's number.

"Mom? Rick again. Yes, she's a lot better, but she has this damn-fool idea that she wants to go home. Do I take her or keep her here?" Rick covered the mouthpiece and leaned into the living room. "Do you live with anyone?" he asked wickedly.

Amy shook her head. "But if I called David, he would probably be glad to come and stay with me." Amy really didn't want David either, but of the two, she felt that David, her fiancé, should be the one to stay with her.

Rick's face became expressionless. "She's going to call her boyfriend," he told his mother tersely. "Thanks, Mom."

Amy got up and wandered into the kitchen. She dialed David's number and waited patiently. On the twentieth ring, he took the receiver from her hand and replaced it into the cradle. "He isn't home," Rick said. "I guess you get to stay here."

"Is it absolutely necessary?" Amy asked crossly to hide her unease. If she stayed here, something that she was not counting on was bound to happen.

"You know better than that," Rick said sternly. "These insect venom reactions are unpredictable. What if it came back up and you were alone? How would you take care of yourself?"

"All right, I'm convinced," Amy said, resigned. She opened the refrigerator door and peered inside. "I'm hungry," she volunteered as she removed a slab of cheese from the meat cooler.

Rick took the hint. "If you'll wait in the living room, I'll make you a sandwich."

Amy obediently returned to the living room. When Rick had first brought her in, she had been too sick to pay much attention to her surroundings, but now she looked around with interest at

114

Rick's home. The furnishings were simple butcher block inter-spersed with genuine primitive antiques not unlike her own, although Rick had fewer, more expensive antiques than she had. Photographs of almost everything imaginable lined the walls, and thick albums of photographs filled a large bookcase. Amy got up and wandered around, examining the pictures. There were nature shots, portraits of interesting faces, stark architec-tural pictures, and several disturbing photographs of a war-torn country that Amy could not readily identify. At that moment Amy realized that Rick Patterson's talent could almost be de-scribed as genius. In spite of what he said about Tommy Lee, there were very few that could equal Rick. It was a thought that pleased her very much.

"Have a sandwich," Rick said as he handed her a heaping plate. She hungrily munched a delicious meat-filled sandwich that could almost be described as a meal in itself. If this sandwich and the spice rack and worn cookbooks in the kitchen were anything to go by, Rick was obviously an accomplished cook. Amy helped herself to another sandwich and washed it down with a tall glass of iced tea. "Thanks," she mumbled. "I was hungry."

"I thought you might be," Rick said wryly. "Now, off to bed for you. It's late."

As Amy made her way to the bathroom she discreetly sur-veyed Rick's town house. Yes, there was a second bedroom, down at the end of the small hall. Once in the bathroom, Amy gratefully stripped off her grimy clothes and gasped in horror at her red, blotched stomach and legs. In the van, she had scratched them raw in her misery, and now the hot shower was making them sting sharply. She soaped herself as gently as she could, then patted herself dry and commandeered a huge cotton bath-robe that hung on a hook behind the door. She realized that she had no gown, but in the state her skin was in, she probably would not have been able to wear one anyway. She wandered down to the spare bedroom, sneaking a peek into Rick's master bedroom and wishing she had the time to snoop around the large, comfortable hideaway, decorated in rich browns. The bed in the small spare room had been turned back, and Amy shed the robe and slipped between the covers gratefully.

"Turn over," Rick ordered from the door as he strode in boldly. In his hand he held a tube of soothing ointment. "Mother just called and suggested this."

"I'll—manage," Amy stammered as she pulled the sheet up to her chin.

"No, you won't," Rick said firmly as he pulled the sheet down to her waist, exposing her small breasts and her blotched stomach to his gaze. "You'll fumble around under the covers and miss half the bad spots."

He pushed Amy back into the pillow and squirted a cold stream of ointment between her breasts and down her stomach. "Yow!" Amy cried as she sat up. "That's cold!" She clutched at the sheet, which had fallen well past any point of modesty.

"Lie down!" Rick ordered tersely as he pushed her back down and rubbed the lotion between Amy's breasts and over her stomach with the flat of his hand. The lotion was indeed soothing to Amy's stinging flesh, but the touch of Rick's hand was creating another kind of itch, this one deep in the core of Amy's femininity. Breathing deeply, she strove to fight the urge she had to throw the ointment across the floor and herself into Rick's arms. She could not possibly feel this kind of longing for one man when she was engaged to another, but she did. She wanted Rick Patterson desperately. From the hooded look in Rick's eyes, she could not tell what he was thinking, but when he ordered her to turn over, she did so gratefully, eager to end the familiar touch of his hands on her breasts and stomach. Perhaps if he was rubbing her back instead of her front, his touch would not seem so erotic, and she could quell the passion that was threatening to erupt between them.

That thought proved to be mistaken. Rick poured another stream of cold ointment into her skin and proceeded to rub it into her back, dipping below the waistline to where the seductive suit had stopped just above her bottom. Then his hand strayed lower, and as Amy arched her back, Rick turned her over and pulled her into his arms, kissing her passionately and rubbing his fingers up and down her spine. "My God, you're a sexy little thing," he moaned as he nibbled her lips with his.

Wordlessly Amy returned his kisses and caresses, teasing his mouth erotically with her tongue, moaning in pleasure when his mouth, sliding down her throat, found one small nipple and tickled it to a proud erection. She arched her back to allow Rick full access to her breast and sucked in her stomach as his mouth gently lowered itself more fully on the hard nipple. He suckled it until it was tense and turgid, then he let his tongue slide to the other nipple, which he nipped unexpectedly with gentle teeth, sending a wave of mild pain and intense pleasure coursing through Amy's body. Sighing, she opened Rick's shirt and teased his chest with her warm, wet lips eliciting a groan of pleasure from him. Withdrawing impatiently, he drew his shirt up over his head and threw it across the floor, then pulled off his pants in one swift movement. His nude body shimmered in the faint light filtering in the window. Amy feasted on the sight of him, tall and proud, then welcomed him with open arms as he stretched out carefully over her, not crushing her sore skin but tickling her delicate breasts with his chest hair. Amy moaned beneath him, arching her body instinctively as she drew her hand down Rick's side and over his quivering stomach. Her hands strayed even lower, finding Rick's hipbones and then sliding her hands around to his hard buttocks. Rick flinched as she touched him there, then relaxed as Amy rotated her fingers in an erotic pattern on his bare skin. "Those little fingers feel so good!" he moaned.

"So do yours, Rick," Amy murmured. "And your mouth!" Rick took the hint and allowed his mouth to return to Amy's breasts and tender throat, then sliding down her chest and back up again, further tormenting her sensitive nipples until she was almost frantic. David was forgotten. Reason was forgotten. For once Amy allowed her body and her emotions to take control of her actions completely, and she reveled in the experience. She was sharing in the most glorious physical expression that she had ever known, and she wanted to experience it all. All she cared about was knowing the possession of the man who was tormenting her with his hands and his lips. She wanted him. He wanted her. And that was all that mattered.

Rick's hands slid down her body and found her narrow hips, which writhed at his touch. Her instinctive movements drove him on as nothing contrived or practiced ever could. "My God, Rick!" Amy moaned helplessly. "I want you!"

Rick moved over Amy and filled her completely, taking her body with all the passion of his being. Amy, shaken by the sensations he was arousing in her, responded instinctively, mindlessly, following Rick's lead with an unerring feel for what was going to happen next. As their emotion spiraled together Rick moaned Amy's name as sweat beaded his brow. Amy buckled upward to meet his passion and stiffened as a storm of pleasure broke over her body, dashing her gloriously into an unknown realm. A similar wave broke over Rick, carrying him over the heights.

"Good?" Rick asked unnecessarily as they lay together in the quiet aftermath.

"Did you need to ask?" Amy said gently as she rubbed his naked chest, loving the feel of the crisp curling hair as it poked impudently up through her fingers. Oh, yes, it had been good. It had been wonderful. Rick had been the perfect lover she had always imagined him to be. She raised her head and kissed him lingeringly on the lips, then absently she ran the back of her hand down Rick's side.

"Damn, that hurt!" Rick yelped as he sat up suddenly. Amy looked at him in dismay, and then down to her hand. In the wild excitement of their passion, David's ring had become twisted at a lethal angle, and she had scratched Rick cruelly down the side.

118

Rick looked derisively down at the ring and, with a savage motion, grabbed Amy's wrist. "Take that damned Cracker Jack trinket off," he ordered.

"No!" Amy ground out savagely. Horrified, she got out from under the sheet, quite unmindful of her own nudity, and wrapped the bathrobe around herself. She stood proudly by the bed while Rick, with trembling fingers, lit a cigarette and inhaled deeply. He looked her in the eye, the contempt he had not quite masked on earlier occasions clearly visible in his eyes and marring his good looks. Stung by his contempt, Amy returned his look with one of scorn. "So you're angry because I won't take off the ring," she spat. "Because I'm engaged to another man and prefer him to you."

"You don't really prefer him, pretty lady, and you know it," Rick snarled. "If you did, you wouldn't have just made love to me the way you did. For once you weren't so stinking high and mighty. You came down off your pedestal and enjoyed some of the things the rest of us less brilliant mortals like."

"All right, damn it, I admit that I liked making love to you. So what? Any female in her right mind would, and you know it, every time you look in the mirror. That doesn't mean I have to throw away a future with David because of it."

"Some future," Rick jeered. "Shop talk at the supper table, insipid sex once a week, two point eight brilliant children. Is that what you want, Amy? To found a dynasty of your own with your brilliant scholar?"

"At least David's man enough to ask a woman to marry him, not to line up outside his door for his favors," Amy returned coldly. "Maybe my kids will have some morals."

"They'll be too dry and dull to have anything else," Rick snorted. "But frankly, Amy, you're not going to marry David and you know it." He leaned back against the pillows and folded his arms. "We both know it. You're too strongly attracted to me. If you had any business marrying him, you wouldn't respond so delightfully when I make love to you." Amy glared at him in

119

pure rage, but he continued speaking, almost calmly at this point. "No, you won't marry him." Rick looked at her confidently.

"What are you going to do to stop me?" Amy jeered. "Kidnap me? Tell him about tonight? Dishonor me with him? What are you planning?"

"I'm not going to do any of those things," Rick said smugly. "I don't need to. You're too smart a lady to marry him. You'll come to your senses without my help. I just wish you had done it before now."

Before Amy could stop him, he pulled her down onto the bed and bore her down into the pillows, ignoring her furious protests, and kissed her until she was moaning. As she arched her body into his, he pulled away abruptly, a look of cruel satisfaction on his face. "Don't forget," he taunted as he left her, closing the door behind him.

Amy stared at the ceiling, her eyes full of tears, for most of the night. A part of her felt bitterly guilty for betraying David the way she had. David was her fiancé, for heaven's sake! Yet another part of her wanted to go down the hall and join Rick in his big bed, and to accept whatever he had to offer her. Amy pounded her pillow with her fist. Oh, how could she ever solve this one? For once Amy's brilliance deserted her, and she was as confused and uncertain as the next woman. Finally, without understanding the significance of her action, she pulled off David's ring and put it in her purse, then turned over and finally went to sleep.

CHAPTER SEVEN

The entire faculty of the biology department was assembled in the conference room, and Amy could feel tension as tight as that in an overwound violin string. Today the new appointment of an associate professor would be announced. Despite David's opinion, Amy thought she had a good chance of receiving the associate professorship but she sincerely hoped that David would be awarded it. Looking across the room, she caught David's eye and winked at him flirtatiously, but he smiled only wanly at her in reply. It's really getting to him, she thought. He really wants that position.

Striding into the room, Dr. Thompson sat down at the head of the large oblong conference table and cleared his throat. The room quietened immediately, and the stragglers quickly filled the empty chairs around the table. Amy glanced around the table at the eager, hopeful faces of the younger faculty members and the speculative faces of the older, more established men and women. They too had been young hopefuls at one time, and now, although they were not affected by today's announcements, they were intensely curious as to who the honored ones would be.

Dr. Thompson quickly dispensed with the routine business of

registration assignments, and then took a piece of paper from his briefcase. It had been freshly typed and bore the unmistakable look of an important document. Oh, please, Amy thought, let me be on the list.

"Now it gives me great pleasure to announce the promotion for next year," Dr. Thompson said. "As you know, we take great pride in the fact that our promotions are made strictly upon merit here at the university by using a point system, thereby eliminating politics and special favors. This year I am proud to announce that we are awarding tenure and the associate professorship to a young professor."

Dr. Thompson stopped and cleared his throat again, enjoying every minute of the suspense he was creating. Here it comes, thought Amy.

"As you all know, we have postponed making the new appointments until very late this year. There was a reason for this. As most of you are aware, a certain percentage of the points awarded by the promotion committee are awarded on the basis of the research project and accompanying publication that the various contenders have completed. This year, one of our faculty members was delayed in completing a project until very late, and has not yet published the completed work. However, on the basis of all other points awarded to this applicant, the committee felt that it would only be fair to read the rough draft of the work and award points to this document. On the basis of that rough draft and the overwhelming points earned in other areas by Dr. Amy Walsh, it gives me great pleasure to announce that the associate professorship will be offered to her. Congratulations, Dr. Walsh!"

Amy sat stunned for a moment while her colleagues applauded her enthusiastically. She was the new associate professor! Automatic tenure and a five thousand dollar raise! She stumbled to her feet, and as the news filtered through to her conscious thoughts, she smiled broadly and stifled an urge to jump up and down in glee. As the applause died down Amy cleared her throat. "Thank you to the committee and to you, Dr. Thompson, for the promotion, and thank you, colleagues, for the help and support. I am very proud to be a part of this institution, and I will do the best job I know how to do."

She sat down to another round of applause, and looked across the room for David. His chair was empty. Puzzled, Amy looked around the room but did not see him. The meeting lasted another few minutes, long enough for Amy's pulse to return to normal, and then she spent a good half hour accepting the sincere congratulations of her colleagues. Finally, as the faculty straggled out of the room, Amy slipped out and walked down the long corridor to her office, noting halfway down the hall that the door was ajar. Knowing she had not left the door open, Amy quickened her pace, concerned that a student might be waiting for her. She walked in to find David sprawled in her spare chair. He sniffed and stuffed a handkerchief in his pocket. "Congratulations, hon. I'm sure you're pleased."

Amy looked at David's bright eyes. What could she say? She was not sorry to have got the appointment, but she was horrified by David's reaction to it. Shaken, she knelt by his chair and took his hand. "I'm really sorry that you're so disappointed. I wish there had been something for you, too."

"Yeah," David said morosely. "So do I."

"There will be another associate position up next year," Amy said soothingly. "I bet that one goes to you."

"Sure," David said quietly. "Damn it, Amy!" he exclaimed suddenly. "It doesn't seem fair! Not when you're going to be quitting in a few years, anyway!"

"I never said that I was quitting," Amy said quietly. Quitting her job would be like cutting off her right arm.

"Of course you are," David exclaimed. "When we have our family I won't permit you to work."

"I wasn't aware that I needed your permission," Amy said spiritedly, withdrawing her hand from his and standing up. "Look, maybe this isn't the time to settle this, but I have no

123

intention of giving up my career when our family comes. We'll both raise the kids and use a responsible caretaker when we both have to be gone. I intend to go just as far in my career as I can."

"That's the most asinine thing I ever heard," David snapped. "You had an edge, you know. They needed to give a promotion to a woman this year."

Amy's voice was dangerously quiet, revealing rather than concealing her anger. "I earned that promotion, and we both know that." Calmly she removed the gaudy ring from her purse and placed it in David's front pocket, then brushed past him and walked down the hall and out the door, her eyes smarting with unshed tears. It's happened again, she thought. Just like before. Way to go, Amy. You get the job, you lose the man. For once she made no attempt to control her emotions, letting the weight of her disappointment sag her shoulders and slow her gait to a shuffle.

Her doorbell rang at eight thirty. Amy left the couch where she had spent the better part of the afternoon and evening and let David in. She gestured to his usual chair and took her place on the couch, but she made no move to turn on the light or speak to David. Nervously he cleared his throat. "Amy, I'm sorry," he said quietly.

"So am I," she replied woodenly.

"I realize that I can't take back what I said, but I didn't really mean it. I know you had that promotion coming," David said.

"Thank you," Amy replied sincerely.

"Will you take back the ring?" David asked slowly.

Amy took a deep breath and expelled it slowly. "No," she said baldly. She felt no emotion but numbness.

"Why?" David demanded. "I apologized about the promotion."

"But, David, it isn't just the promotion. It's a lot of other things, too. Things like we don't want the same thing out of a marriage." She held up her hand as David started to speak. "No, hear me out. You want a wife that will fit into your preconceived

124

niche. A woman who will fill society's role of the contented homemaker and mother. I can't do that. I have to keep working, keep using my brain, or I'll go crazy."

"So keep working," David said. "I'll get used to it."

"But what about the next time I get the promotion and you don't? We both have to admit that I'm a better teacher and researcher than you and that I'm likely to go farther than you. Is it going to eat out your insides over the years as this happens? Will you end up hating me?"

"We have a lot going for us," David reminded her.

"But we have a lot against us, too," she said softly, shaking her head.

"Yeah," David said with frustration as he got up and paced the floor. "I don't have that something that puts a sweet blush on your face. I can't make you smile when you don't realize that anyone is looking. I can't make you dreamy-eyed in the middle of the day." David looked down at the ring in his palm. "I couldn't make you take off some other fellow's ring. If I could, I'd say to hell with your promotion, my insecurities. But I can't do all those things, so I won't insist."

Amy stared at him aghast. "David, I'm sorry," she whispered, tears welling in her eyes and running down her cheeks. She put her head in her hands and sobbed brokenly as David sat beside her on the couch and held her close. She cried for her own broken dreams, and for the hurt she had caused David, the man she loved but not in the right way. Finally her storm of tears subsided, leaving her drained and spent. "I'm sorry," she whispered again. "I never meant to hurt you."

"You had no control over it. Tell me, do you have any kind of future with him?"

"No," Amy said flatly. "He's a philanderer."

"Ouch," David said.

"Oh, I'll be all right," Amy said sadly. "I'll get myself a cat." In spite of the anguish she felt, she smiled wanly into the gloom.

David reached over and kissed Amy sadly, then he walked out

the front door and pulled it shut behind him, leaving her alone in the deepening darkness.

So her love for Rick had been obvious to David, even before it was clear to her. Now she understood why she had resisted wearing David's ring since the night she had spent with Rick. She couldn't wear one man's ring while she loved another. All right, she told herself. You love him. What are you going to do about it? Amy sat up until midnight, thinking and twisting her ring, but still she did not know when she finally went to bed.

Amy gazed thoughtfully at the computer console behind Betty Jean's desk. In the entire two months she had been working at Patterson's, to her knowledge no one had ever had the time or the inclination to tackle the machine and make it work. Due to a typical summer flood, most of the jobs for the afternoon had been canceled and the staff had gone on home to avoid the rising floodwaters, leaving Amy to answer the telephone and wait for some of the water to run off. Amy could hear the rain slacking off, but it would be several hours before the low water crossings on the way to her apartment would go down, and she was just as content to stay here at Patterson's. Since she had broken her engagement, she had spent entirely too much time cooped up there, grading papers and working frantically on the final draft of her book.

Amy looked at the console again, and on an impulse she reached for the owner's manual and opened it beside the keyboard. Soon she was busily punching in different things, and the computer was talking back to her on the screen. Delighted with the new toy, she sat mesmerized and punched away happily, quickly working her way through the simple exercises and moving through the manual to more difficult problems. So absorbed was she in her work, she did not hear the front door open or the man enter the room until a large hand fall heavily on her shoulder. Amy leaped around in fright, which soon turned to breathless anticipation when she looked up into Rick's face. She remembered the intimacies that they had shared that night a month ago at his home and the pleasure she had taken in them, and she blushed even as she longed to feel Rick's hard body against hers as she had then. Had he thought of her in a sensual way since then? Thinking of Samantha, she quickly transformed the anticipation into irritation as a measure of self-defense. "Why did you scare me like that?" she demanded crossly.

"Sorry," Rick said unrepentantly. "I made plenty of noise coming in, but you didn't hear me. What have you been doing to my computer?"

Amy stuck out her tongue at him. "I think I've learned enough about programming it to set up your bookkeeping on here," she said. "Go get me your ledger."

"But that takes a special program," Rick protested.

"You bought the program when you bought the computer," Amy replied. "The ledger, please."

Rick got up and brought her back the ledger. Amy opened it to the accounts and was soon feeding numbers into the machine as fast as she could type. Rick watched in awe as she set up the records for July in just a matter of minutes. When she was through punching in information, she fed the machine a command, and the printer that was stationed by the computer begin to whir and then to type out the billing for July.

"I didn't know you could use a computer," Rick said impatiently. "Why didn't you tell me you could? You could have done this two months ago."

"But I couldn't until this afternoon," Amy protested as she examined the printout. She went back to the machine and typed in a few more figures and a new command, and the printer began to whir again. Noting Rick's disbelieving expression, she protested again. "Honestly, I picked up the manual and started doodling with it this afternoon. There was nothing else to do." She picked up the manual and turned to the place where she had left off. It was about three quarters of the way through the book.

Rick looked at the book and whistled unbelievingly. "My

127

God, you taught yourself most of BASIC in three hours. It takes most people an entire semester of college to learn that much." He looked at her piercingly, realizing for the first time the true mental giant she was.

Amy shrugged. "It's not hard once you get the hang of it," she said.

"Okay, teach, you show me how the fool thing works," he said with a challenge.

Amy vacated the seat in front of the terminal and motioned for Rick to sit down. She took the chair next to him and spent the next two hours showing Rick what she had learned that afternoon. Although admittedly he did not learn it as quickly as she had, he was a good student and certainly learned more than most people could have in two hours. When they finally called a halt Rick reached out and touched her face gently. "You're a fantastic teacher," he said admiringly. "And you're so damned smart it's scary."

Amy flinched. She did not want to be reminded of that. "Thanks," she said stiffly. "Any time." The rain had stopped, but the clouds obscured the sunset that usually poured in the windows this time of day. Amy left the office quickly, but not before Rick could see the tears in her eyes, leaving him wondering what on earth he had said that hurt her so much.

Amy pulled the brush through her hair listlessly and applied a little extra cover stick to the circles under her eyes. The combined inner turmoil over her promotion and her break with David, and the mental exertion of writing the final draft of her book, were beginning to show in her face. A number of sleepless nights were piling up, and she was tense and edgy. Then too she was confused. Try as she might, she could not help but be excited about the promotion, even though it had cost her a fiancé. The new responsibilities and teaching assignments would challenge her abilities, and that thrilled her. Yet another part of her bitterly regretted the break with David and the bittersweet reason for it.

David had definitely been right. She had no business marrying him, feeling the way she did about Rick, but with Rick she had no future. He had probably even forgotten the lovemaking that Amy relived with regularity in the wee hours of the morning. She looked at herself in the mirror and grimaced. Feeling the way she did about Rick, it was doubtful that she would ever make a decent wife for anyone else. "Oh, well," she said to herself, "you're old maid material if anyone ever was. Quit bellyaching about what you wish had been and go find yourself a cat."

Knowing this time in advance that Rick was shooting a wedding, she made it a point to be ready on time. She had worked with Joe and Tommy Lee on several other weddings, but this was the first with Rick since the wedding with the drunken groom so many weeks ago.

She handed Rick her keys and lip gloss at the door, then walked with him quietly to the car. He glanced sharply at her tired, strained face but said nothing about it, talking with her about the pictures he was to take in the laboratory next week. Amy discussed those enthusiastically for a few minutes, then grew silent for the remainder of the drive to the church, a lovely stone chapel a few miles outside of town.

The wedding was a joy to attend. The bride and groom, a lovely Mexican-American couple in their mid-twenties, intended to work the ranch that had been in the groom's family for nearly a hundred years. Although the families were clearly wealthy, the couple had none of the superficiality or snobbery that characterized so many children of wealthy families. And they were so in love! The deep respect and affection that they gave to each other was truly inspiring. They looked into each other's eyes and repeated their vows with sincerity and intense purpose, and when they kissed at the end of the ceremony, it was with warm, sweet passion, promising a wild and wondrous night to come. Amy stifled her jealousy of the happy couple as she offered her congratulations to them. The families seemed pleased by the union, and the father of the bride invited Rick and Amy to make themselves part of the party that was to come.

As was frequently the custom in the Mexican-American community, a barbecue dinner and dance on the grounds of the church took the place of a formal reception. The barbecue was delicious, especially so to Amy, since she had eaten much earlier in the day, and the cup of cold beer that Rick thrust in her hand was totally refreshing. She finished the cup and asked for another. By the time the grand march had started, Amy was ready for a third.

The band was loud and the dancing lively. Popular tunes were alternated with traditional polkas and *cúmbias,* and to Amy's surprise Rick proved to be an excellent dancer. He was equally adept at fast modern dancing and the traditional Mexican dances, leading the light-footed Amy through the intricate steps of the traditional dances well enough that Amy's lack of expertise at those did not show. Between fast dances they sipped beer and talked companionably, and Amy consumed several more cups of the cold keg beer during the course of the evening. For the slow numbers, he held her tightly to his broad chest, and Amy could feel his breath stir her hair in the soft August night. David, her promotion, and the problems that she was facing were banished to the back of her mind, so potent was the thrill of dancing with the man she loved so much. They stayed and danced with the party long after the bride and groom had left, holding each other close and swaying to the music. It was balm to Amy's wounded spirit.

Finally Rick led Amy off the dance floor and packed his camera bag. Amy thanked their host and hostess, who were delighted that Amy and Rick had stayed and danced. When Amy complimented her hostess on the joyous wedding, the woman smiled delightedly. "Yes, Juan and Sylvia were made for each other. Just as you and your husband seem so happy together."

"Oh, Rick's not my husband," Amy said quickly. "I only work for him."

"No, Amy's not married, but she's almost got one caught," Rick said behind her.

Amy paled in the dim light. "Not anymore," she whispered in an angry hiss.

Their hostess looked confused for a moment, but smiled graciously and thanked Rick again as they said their good-byes and left. Amy sat frozen and angry during the drive back into town. The lovely evening had been spoiled for her. Rick sat tight-lipped and wary until he had parked outside Amy's apartment, but as she jumped out of the car and ran to her apartment, he followed close on her heels. She inserted her key in the lock and gave it a vicious twist, but before she could get the door open, Rick's hand closed over her wrist. "For God's sake, what did I say?" he snarled. "I just told her that you were engaged."

"That was a mean thing to say," Amy shot back, twisting her wrist futilely in his tight grip. "Especially when you know that David and I broke our engagement nearly three weeks ago."

Rick dropped her wrist and pushed her inside the apartment. He took her by the shoulders and sat her gently on the sofa, then sat down in the chair that David had usually occupied and stared into Amy's tired eyes. "No, Amy, I didn't know."

"How could you help but know?" Amy asked bitterly. "I haven't worn the ring since—well—I haven't worn it in awhile."

"I don't notice things like that," Rick said sincerely. "I thought it would happen, but I didn't think it would be so soon."

"And I bet you're tickled pink," Amy said sarcastically. "Well, go ahead. Rub it in. I had enough sense not to marry him. The great Rick Patterson was right again."

"That's the last time I let you loose around a beer keg!" Rick said half indignantly as he observed her flushed cheeks and angry expression. "I do believe you drank too much!"

"And why do you think that?" Amy asked owlishly.

"The mere fact that you think I'd be happy that you're unhappy," Rick said gently. "I'll freely admit that I thought you had no business marrying David, but the break has obviously upset you a great deal. Why, Amy, when you really didn't love him?"

"You're right, I didn't love him that way," Amy responded honestly. "But on another level I did. I was fond of him. We thought we could have a good life together."

"You admit that you were willing to settle for that?" Rick asked incredulously. "Why, Amy, when you have so much to offer?"

"Too damn much, you mean," she exclaimed bitterly. "Look, I admit that David didn't set me on fire. You could tell that even before you and I—" Amy swallowed. "But he wanted to marry me and raise a family together. I want to get married and have children as well as pursue a career. David asked me to do that."

Rick looked at her oddly. "Is that why you were so eager to marry him? Because he wanted to marry you?" Amy nodded. "That's a hell of a reason to marry a man."

"You don't understand," Amy said patiently, as though speaking to one of her students. "I don't have the same choice of men that most women have."

"Why not?" Rick challenged.

"Because of my career," she replied. "No, let's be honest, Rick. Because of my brain. Because of my intellect. It wouldn't have mattered what field I entered. It could have been medicine, or law, or business. The end result would have been the same. I have a choice of only one or two percent of the male population, those whose intellect is competitive with mine. The rest of the men out there are either scared to death around me, afraid of revealing a less than Mensa level IQ, or they get belligerent, because they feel insecure."

"That is the biggest bunch of melodramatic horse manure that I have ever heard," Rick snorted. "Sure, some of the men out there behave that way, but did you ever stop to think that maybe an equal number of men are turned on by the thought of a brilliant woman? Men who would appreciate your sharp mind?"

"Name one man that you know who is turned on by the thought of a brainy woman," Amy challenged.

"I can name you four," Rick said. "Dad, my two brothers, and myself. And the smarter, the better. Now, don't start to protest that we're unique," Rick said as Amy started to speak. "There are a number of men out there who would be delighted to marry you. Would you be interested in a ordinary man, Amy?" He looked at her searchingly.

"Of course I would," Amy replied sincerely. "An ordinary man would suit me just fine." Or a certain one would, she amended to herself.

"I admit that it will take a special man to live with you," Rick added. "He will have to understand your ambition and your drive, and learn not to be intimidated by your intellect. But there's one out there, I'm sure of it. So cheer up. It's going to get better!"

Rick left his chair and sat down beside Amy. She looked into his eyes, desperately wanting to believe him. Wordlessly he nodded his head, and she smiled. Leaning over slowly, he kissed Amy firmly, but with none of the wild passion that had so characterized their earlier fiery embraces. This kiss was meant to comfort, to console, to offer support, and it did just that. As Rick pulled away Amy took his face in her palms and traced the circles under his eyes with her thumbs. "Thank you, Rick. Thank you!"

Rick leaned over and kissed her again, this time with so much passion that it left Amy breathless. Silently he pulled away from her and left her apartment, shutting her front door behind him. About halfway to his car he turned around and looked back up at her window. "God, Amy," he said out loud. "How can you think that an ordinary man wouldn't want you?" He shook his head. "How can you think a thing like that?"

Amy stared at the closing front door. Rick had been so sure that things would get better for her, that someone would want to marry her someday. Someone would want her, Rick was sure of it. Amy stared out the window at Rick's vanishing taillights. Why couldn't it be Rick himself? Oh, God, she thought as she covered her face with her hands. Why couldn't it be Rick who wanted her? She certainly wanted him! Amy allowed herself a few moments of fantasy, thinking about what life would be like being wanted by an impetuous man like him. It would be fun, exhilarating, fulfilling. It would be challenging. It would be wonderful.

Amy twisted the ring on her finger and touched her lips. Grudgingly she gave up her fantasy, remembering Samantha. Life with Rick would have been all sorts of wonderful things. But life with Rick would never be.

CHAPTER EIGHT

Amy looked up from the microscope and rubbed her eyes wearily, then pushed the hair out of her eyes with shaking hands. "The parasite moved out of viewing range. How I don't know. I'll have to start over."

Rick looked around the deserted laboratory and over to the exhausted woman. He frowned as he noted the dark circles under her eyes and the pinched brittleness of her features. "It's after eleven now," he said. "We've done enough tonight."

"I'm going to set up a new slide and try again," she said. "I need the pictures of these by Friday."

"And according to whom do you need the pictures?" Rick asked. "Monday or Tuesday would be soon enough."

"No, it wouldn't," Amy said crossly. "I need to finish this tonight." She turned away and removed the slide from the microscope.

"This is ridiculous," Rick said firmly. "I'm going home."

"Please, I really need to get this done now," Amy pleaded as she clutched at his arm. "I have to work on the book tomorrow night, and you have a wedding to shoot."

Shrugging, Rick stationed himself on a lab stool and watched as Amy opened a sick mussel and removed a small section of the gill. She took a clean slide and placed a razor-thin section of the gill on it, then squirted on a biological stain and waved the slide gently in the air until it was almost dry. She squirted on another stain and repeated the process, then covered the specimen with a cover slip and placed it on the microscope. She added the immersion oil that would permit the very high magnification that she needed and clipped the slide to the stage. Gingerly she lowered the lens onto the cover slip until the lens was just into the oil.

Rubbing her aching back, she bent over the microscope and peered into the eyepiece. After focusing as best she could, she began the painstaking process of searching the slide for a parasite. Although the mussel had a serious infection of the disease, the organisms were not that close together in the flesh, and a sample might or might not have a parasite in the tissue. Amy moved the slide back and forth as smoothly as she could, but under the high-powered magnification, even her slightest movement lurched across the view, straining her eyes and her nerves even further. Amy searched futilely for fifteen minutes but found no parasites. Swearing loudly, she yanked the slide off the stage and threw it on the counter, then prepared a new slide and snapped it into the scope. She added the required oil but misjudged the distance to the lens, screwing it down too far and shattering the cover slip. Oil poured down into the sample and ruined it completely.

Completely exasperated, Amy let loose with a stream of language that would have made a sailor blush. Rick glanced over at the opening door and winked. "Have you ever heard such language coming from a lady?" he asked as Dr. Thompson walked in.

"And in such interesting combinations!" Dr. Thompson replied.

"How long have you been standing there listening?" Amy snapped sharply, too tired to see the humor in the situation.

"I didn't have to stand there," Dr. Thompson replied. "I could hear you from the office."

"Sorry," Amy mumbled. She turned back to the microscope and jerked the ruined slide off the stage. "It's almost midnight and too late to start another one," she muttered tiredly. "Sorry I kept you, Rick."

"Why are you here so late, Amy?" Dr. Thompson asked. "I was finishing a set of papers, but I don't have to teach tomorrow. You do."

"Trying to finish these damned pictures," she replied shortly as she threw the ruined slide into the trash with shaking fingers. Dr. Thompson and Rick exchanged looks, then they walked out into the hall, talking quietly while Amy got ready to go. She cleaned up the messy oil and put away the microscope, then picked up her purse and Rick's camera case and left the laboratory, locking the door behind her.

Dr. Thompson and Rick broke off their conversation, and Rick took the camera bag from her. "Amy, I hate to ask you, but can you come with me tomorrow afternoon on a short job? I really need the help."

Amy nodded reluctantly. She did have to work on the final draft of the book, but then she had kept him here until almost midnight. "Sure," she said, shrugging her slumped shoulders.

"I'll pick you up here after your class," he said smoothly.

"Good night, you two," Dr. Thompson said as he shook Rick's hand. Solemnly, but with a twinkle in his eye, he said, "See you tomorrow, Amy." He looked distinctly amused about something, but Amy was too tired to wonder what.

She wished Rick good night and drove home in the light night traffic. She showered quickly and fell into bed, and there, as she had for too many nights, she tossed and turned, mental and emotional strain preventing the slumber that she needed. At first she thought about the final draft of her book. She was almost finished, but the book was not as good as she had hoped that it would be. She thought about the things that she would change

137

and promised herself that she would smooth out the rough places. But inevitably her thoughts turned to Rick. Damn! Why had she gone and fallen in love with him? She figured that she had probably loved him from the beginning, otherwise she would not have responded to his lovemaking the way that she had. And a fat lot of good it did her. She had been forced to give up her plans to marry David, and Rick could offer her no more than a one-night stand. She punched her pillow and thrashed around in her narrow bed. Would unsatisfied longing for Rick keep her awake every night for the rest of her life?

Amy fell into an uneasy sleep a little before dawn and then overslept. Showering and dressing quickly, she ran out the door and banged it behind her. She slammed her car into gear and drove away quickly, not noticing the van parked halfway down the block.

She made it to the university in time to teach her class, but was sharp with her students and had to look up the answer to a simple question. When the bell finally rang she watched the class file out and then sat down at one of the desks, cradling her head in her hand.

"Are you ready to go?" Rick asked as he poked his head around the door and grinned especially wickedly. Amy nodded wearily and followed him out to the van, parked in direct violation of the campus parking policies. Rick ripped the ticket off of the windshield and handed it to Amy. "Fix that, will you?" he asked as he helped her inside the van and locked the door firmly behind her.

Rick started the engine and drove off the campus to the nearest freeway entrance. Amy wondered where the job was but did not care enough to ask. Rick picked up speed and they drove north, through the northside commercial section and then through prosperous residential neighborhoods. Amy glanced back and saw only one camera case. "The job today must be pretty small," she said idly. "You don't have much equipment."

"Yes, it's a small job," Rick agreed. "Small but important."

138

They drove on through the suburbs, then Rick took another exit and got on the same highway that led to the lakes. "How much farther to the job?" Amy asked. "I need to get back and work on the book."

"About a hundred miles or so," Rick said blandly.

"A hundred miles! That's all the way to the lakes! We won't be back until late tonight!" Amy fumed.

"Correction, Amy." Rick laughed. "We won't be back for several days. There isn't any job. I'm kidnapping you."

"You can't do that!" Amy sputtered angrily as she whirled around to face him. "You turn around and take me right back home! I have a lot of work to do."

"No way," Rick said calmly. "That's exactly why I'm spiriting you away. You've been working too hard and your production has fallen off. You're going to relax for a few days with me up at Dr. Thompson's cabin, then you're going home to write the best damned book that university has ever published."

"But what about your job? My teaching?"

"Tommy Lee and Joe can cover for me, and Dr. Thompson asked Jack Morgan to cover for you." Rick looked at her tense, angry face and dropped the light tone of voice he had been using. "You need a break before you do break, and I'm going to see that you get it. And you can blame Dr. Thompson for half of this. He offered me the cabin if I would just do it."

"I intend to speak to him," Amy said sharply, but she admitted to herself that the men were right. She was near the breaking point, but how could she relax at the cabin with Rick there? She chewed her fingernail and stared out the window. Ever since she had realized her love for him, she had been careful not to say or do anything that would betray her heart to him. How would she be able to keep up the pretense for several days?

"What am I supposed to wear for the next few days?" Amy asked crossly.

"Oh, that's no problem," Rick replied smoothly. "Your land-

139

lady let me in this morning after you left. I packed enough clothes to last you a few days. I thought of everything."

They drove in silence for a number of miles, Amy resigning herself to the fact that she would be staying with Rick in the small house. How would they get along in the confined space with no work to do? Although by now they had made a number of visits to the cabin, they had always been so busy that they seldom had time to do anything but work. But Rick had finished his pictures at the lake sites several weeks ago, and this time there was nothing to fill the hours. Amy stared out the window at the cedar-covered hills, a little dry this time of the year but nevertheless beautiful, and wondered how they would pass the time.

Rick stopped off in Johnson City, and they bought groceries. Amy protested that he was buying much too much for just a few days, until he reminded her that he ate almost as much as she did. Thus armed, they drove to the cabin, chatting pleasantly about various things, and Amy felt her anger at her abduction fading. Maybe Rick and Dr. Thompson knew what they were doing. Already she felt better.

It was almost supper time when they arrived at the cabin. Rick volunteered to cook supper if she would get the suitcases from the van. Amy agreed, noting with satisfaction that Rick had packed her cosmetics as well as her clothes, and that he had included one nice pair of pink slacks and a matching top. She walked into the kitchen and sniffed appreciatively. *"Fajitas?"* she asked eagerly.

Rick removed the juicy skirt steaks from the broiler and basted them with hot sauce. "It's easy to do in a hurry," he explained. Without being told, Amy found the ripe avocados on the counter and mashed them, adding a dash of hot sauce to make it a spicy guacamole, then she chopped tomatoes and peppers into a tongue-burning *picadillo* while Rick warmed the tortillas. Contentedly they stuffed first the tortillas and then themselves, licking the juicy concoction from their lips and washing it down with beer. Amy proclaimed Rick the cook for the duration of the stay, but he declined, pointing out that no one could equal her when it came to stew. They washed up the dishes and Rick suggested a walk on the lakeshore, a suggestion that Amy agreed with wholeheartedly.

They wandered down the beach, holding hands and frolicking in the shallow water of the sandy shore. Rick picked up several large mussel shells that had washed up, and Amy put them in her pocket. When they had wandered far down the shore Rick motioned to a fallen log, and they sat and watched the sunset together. Dipping low in the sky, the sun seemed to hesitate a moment before it fell below the horizon, shining for one more moment of glory before continuing on its journey. Amy watched, mesmerized, feeling the tension of the past weeks draining from her mind and her body. As the sky grew darker the stars winked on one by one, spangling the night sky like a giant crown of jewels. Rick slipped his arm around Amy and drew her to him slowly, cupping her pliant body into his own and kissing her hungrily. Amy responded mindlessly, loving the feel of his body and his lips on her own. Rick pulled back from her and drew her up. "It's time we went back," he said. "I brought you up here to rest, and I'm going to see that you do just that."

When Amy returned to the main room from the shower, she found Rick in the kitchen, mixing an interesting-looking drink. "What's that?" she asked as she reached in the refrigerator for her usual glass of milk.

"This is for you," Rick said as he handed her the glass. "It's a Rick Patterson special. Guaranteed to delight the senses."

Amy sniffed the mixture and sipped it tentatively. "It's delicious!" she exclaimed. "What's in it?"

"All kinds of things," Rick said cheerfully. "Rum, fruit juice, several spices. My own secret recipe."

Rick poured a drink for himself and carried his out to the main room. Amy followed him and sat down on her daybed. Rick picked up a magazine and sat down in the big chair in the corner.

He nonchalantly leafed through the magazine while Amy watched him through her eyelashes. Had he brought her here to make love to her again? Did she want to make love to him again? Turning her back to the room, Amy sipped her drink and stared out the window at the lake, calm tonight and silvered by the light of the moon. Should she ask Rick if he intended to start an affair with her? No, that would be going a bit too far, especially since she had no idea what his feelings were for her, other than that he desired her. She finished her drink in several large swallows and lay down on the pillows to think for hours as she had for so many nights in the past.

Five minutes later, Rick heard the sound of the quiet, even breathing that told him that Amy was asleep. He smiled to himself. Patterson's special worked every time. He waited a few more minutes to be sure that she was really asleep, then leaned over her and kissed her gently on the mouth. "Good night, pretty lady," he whispered as he returned to the easy chair and picked up his magazine.

Amy woke to the sound of the back door slamming shut. She sat up and rubbed her eyes, trying to get her bearings, and saw that the sun was high in the sky. Rick was dripping across the room, leaving a trail of wet, sandy footprints behind him. "Morning, pretty lady," he drawled in a exaggerated imitation of John Wayne. "It's almost noon. Care to get up now?"

"Almost noon! I'm sorry!" Amy yelped as she leaped off the daybed.

"Don't apologize," Rick said firmly. "You needed the rest. I have a picnic basket ready. We're going for a ride."

Thirty minutes later they were in the boat again, but this time instead of seeking out mussel beds, they were motoring up the lake to the falls, a natural waterfall that spilled into the lake and could only be reached by boat. Rick skillfully avoided the dead tree trunks that had calcified under the surface of the water and now were a menace to anyone in a motorboat and anchored the boat in the middle of the cove. Hungrily Amy consumed enough sandwiches to put even Rick to shame, then lay back on the hull of the boat and let the hot sun beat into her flesh. "You know, I'm ruining my skin," Amy said, "but the feel of the sun is so good to me."

Rick looked at her critically. "Your skin looks fine to me," he said. "Every inch of it is great."

"Very funny," Amy muttered as she flopped over. "This would be a great place to swim, and I'm hot. I wish I'd brought my suit."

Rick looked around. "No reason why we can't swim here," he said lightly. "There's no one around to see us."

"You mean skinny-dip?" Amy asked, tempted by the thought.

"Why not?" Rick asked reasonably. "There's no one around. Come on, Amy. I dare you!"

Amy's adventurous spirit that had laid dormant for so long rose at long last with a vengeance. "You don't think I'll really do it," she accused Rick. "Well, I sure as hell will!" She laughed as she sat up. Swiftly she wiggled out of her T-shirt and bra, and without a moment's hesitation she slipped out of her shorts and panties and stood naked on the hull. "Okay, Rick. Your turn," she said as he stared at her, an astonished look on his face.

"I didn't think you would really do it," he muttered as he pulled the T-shirt over his head. In seconds he was as naked as she was, his magnificent body completely bared to the hot summer sun. Amy dove into the cool green water of the lake, and Rick followed her.

Amy struck out and swam all of ten feet before Rick caught up with her. He reached out and poked her head under the surface of the water. Gasping, Amy surfaced and retaliated by shoving a fistful of water into Rick's face. Grinning, he reached out and drew her to him slowly. "I have to pay you back for that," he murmured wickedly as their naked limbs tangled under the water.

"That's not fair," Amy whispered with a lump in her throat. The cool water lapped around their nude bodies. "You started

143

it." She said no more as Rick's mouth came down on her own, at first in playful punishment and then, as the nature of the kiss changed, with burgeoning excitement. Amy clung to him and tangled her feet up in his legs, not even letting go when they sank slowly below the surface of the water. Finally, just as Amy was about to run out of air, Rick released her and together they drifted to the surface. Amy stared at Rick, not wanting to break the spell.

He reached out and kissed her gently on the nose, his hair trailing down into his eyes. "Race you to the falls," he challenged her with a grin.

"You're on!" Amy responded gaily, striking out toward the long, high falls that were plunging into the lake.

Rick let her get a third of the way there, then plunged his head under the water and swiftly caught up with Amy, passing her easily. He was waiting behind the falls when Amy arrived there. "Me thinks you are a show-off," she commented dryly.

Rick shrugged. "Swimming has always come naturally to me," he said as he reached for Amy. She thought he intended to kiss her again, but instead he pulled her behind the falls and motioned to some odd-looking plant growth on the rocks behind the falls. "What are those?" he asked.

"A peculiar kind of primitive water plant. The exact species name escapes me for the moment," she admitted. "Aren't they fascinating?" Amy looked with a trained eye at the unusual plant species that dwelt behind the falls, protected from the hot, drying Texas sun. Some of these species probably could not be found anywhere else on the lake.

Amy's mind wandered from the plants behind the falls to the man who was treading water beside her. Would they ever make love again? Did she want to? She looked out from behind the curtain of water at the lake and the hills. She felt that there behind the waterfall, she and Rick were the only two people in the world. They were in a cocoon of water that shut out everything else. Impulsively she turned to Rick. He was looking at her intently, his eyes burning like coals and his naked body a sensual invitation. "Kiss me again, Rick . . ." she murmured softly.

Rick reached out and pulled her through the water until their bodies were touching. He held the upper part of her body close to his, leaving their legs free to tread water, and kissed her, his tongue gliding in and around the sensitive lining of her mouth, as he held her tightly around the waist with one hand. Amy ran her hand down his side, cool from his prolonged contact with the cold lake water, and down his muscled thigh, causing the deep arousal within him to become evident. The water of the lake lapped their heated bodies as they touched each other's most intimate centers of desire, and the spray from the falls misted their faces and their hair. With his powerful free arm, Rick was able to keep them afloat as they drowned, not in water, but in the heady sharing of passionate emotion.

When Rick finally released Amy they both were trembling. They swam out from behind the falls slowly, as though unwilling to rejoin the rest of the world, but once they were back out in the body of the lake, Rick reached out and dunked Amy again, and she reached out and caught his leg, pulling him down with her. Naked and laughing, they teased and tussled with one another until they both were exhausted.

"Swimming naked really is better," she said an hour later as they sat nude in the boat, waiting for their bodies to dry enough to put on their clothes.

"I agree," Rick said as he lay on the hull, eyeing her thoughtfully. Amy's gaze rested on the naked male body that had been at the forefront of her thoughts for the last hour. The bedroom had been darkened the night they had made love, and Amy had not seen Rick clearly, but the sun was bright on the lake, and she could see Rick completely today. She was devastated by his masculinity. Rick was absolutely gorgeous in the nude, with perfectly proportioned muscles gleaming in the sun, and his casual acceptance of his manly body added to his attractiveness both as a sexy man and as a person. As though looking for flaws, Amy peered down at her own small body.

"Amy, I want you to do something for me," Rick said quietly as he gazed at her naked form.

"Sure, Rick, what do you want?" Amy said absently.

"I want you to pose for me in the nude," he said quickly. As Amy turned startled eyes to him, he rushed on. "I was kidding that day in the coffee shop, but I'm not now. You have a beautiful body, one that I would like to record on film if I may. And, no, I don't say this to every woman I know," he said sharply at Amy's cynical look. "You're the first woman in years, other than professional models, that I have wanted to photograph."

Amy thought for a minute. Skinny-dipping with Rick was one thing, but posing naked? She was certainly not offended by nudity, but did she have the nerve to pose in front of Rick's all-seeing lens? She looked at Rick's expectant face and realized that he really did want her to pose for him. At that point her adventurous spirit took over completely. "When and where?" she asked wickedly.

Rick smiled slowly. "If you mean it, and I think you really do, we'll go back to the house and you can dry your hair and put on a little makeup. Then I want to take you outdoors—maybe I'll photograph you under a canopy of trees. You belong outside." Rick pulled on his clothes and threw Amy hers. "Put these on before your backside burns," he commanded.

Amy washed and dried her hair, brushing it until it shone, and lightly made up her face, covering the circles under her eyes with a cover stick, although the shadows were much lighter than they had been just the day before. She slipped into a pair of shorts and a shirt and followed Rick as he returned to the boat. "I remember the perfect spot for this," he volunteered as he headed the boat back out onto the water. "It's on the island out there."

Rick parked the boat, and Amy followed him as he quickly searched the island, making sure that they had it to themselves.

146

He then walked into the interior of the small island to a spot where the trees furnished a natural canopy over the sky, not casting a deep shade but gently dappling the earth with light and shadow. He spread the blanket that Amy had carried for him and unpacked a camera and loaded it. Amy watched him with much of her adventurous spirit melting away. Had she really agreed to pose nude for him? Looking up, Rick caught the look of uncertainty on her face and smiled at her. "Don't disappoint me, pretty lady," he said softly. "You look so beautiful."

Amy unbuttoned her blouse slowly, then pulled off her bra and dropped them both into the grass. Slowly she removed her shorts and panties until she stood before him, naked and unashamed. "I'm not beautiful," she said softly, "but if you want to take my picture, I would be proud for you to do so."

Rick walked over to her and sat her down on the blanket. He handed her a wispy robe that she did not know he had brought with him, and helped her put her arms through it. "I want a picture of you in this first," he said softly as he arranged the folds so that her body was unveiled in sensual invitation. With shaking hands, Rick mounted his camera on a small tripod and focused it, then stood to one side as he talked to Amy. "Talk to me, pretty lady," he cajoled. "Seduce me with your eyes. No, not like that," he admonished as Amy gave him her best come-hither look. "You look like a hooker."

"Gee, thanks," Amy snapped as she sat up indignantly, her small body quivering in aggravation.

"Sorry," Rick said unrepentantly. Amy smiled at him wickedly. "That's the look I want!" Rick yelped as he shot four pictures in rapid succession. "You look like the cat that ate the canary." He told her to turn her head to the side. "A woman who's about to make love is supposed to look very satisfied."

"I thought we were supposed to look satisfied after we made love," Amy returned, allowing the robe to slide from her shoulders. She sat up and breathed in deeply, her small breasts thrust forward proudly, a sincerely sensual smile on her face.

"Well, then, too," Rick admitted as he snapped more pictures. Pausing to change film, he instructed Amy to take off the robe. She slid out of it and tossed it to one side, stretching like a kitten as she laid down on the blanket. "That's good," Rick said as he remounted the camera and took several more pictures. "Stretch again for me."

The look Rick gave her was blatantly sensual, and Amy felt her body respond, her nipples growing hard and full, although he had not even touched her. She stretched again and again, looking and finding desire in Rick's eyes. He walked over to her and rolled her over gently, although his hands seared Amy where they touched her. "Now look back at me," he commanded. "I want a picture of you looking over your shoulder, like the one I took at Fort Wilson." Amy obediently duplicated that position.

"No mosquitos today," she quipped as Rick took the last picture of her in that pose.

Rick came to her again and turned her on her side. "Prop your head on your hand," he commanded, bending her elbow and lightly grazing her breast with his hand. Amy sucked in her breath at the exquisite sensation. Tearing himself away, Rick focused the camera and took several pictures, then swore softly and returned to Amy, sitting down beside her and taking her into his arms. He kissed her as he wound his arms around her slender body. "Amy, I want to make love to you, but I don't want it to be like the time before, when you were angry with me afterward. This time I'm asking, Amy. What do you say?" His grip tightened as he waited for her to say yes or no.

Amy did neither. Forgetting David, forgetting Samantha, forgetting Linda, forgetting everything except the feel of Rick's body against hers and the love she felt for him in her heart, she reached up and pulled his mouth down to hers, nibbling and tasting his lips with her own. The sunlight filtering through the trees dappled their faces and Amy's naked body, and the crickets sang a love medley for the two of them. Rick responded instantly to Amy's caressing kisses, pushing her down on the blanket and covering her body with his. Amy could feel the evidence of his desire against her, exciting her as no declarations of passion could have. She arched her body up to his, feeling her naked breasts strain against the soft fabric of his T-shirt, her hips against the rough fabric of his jeans. "Your clothes feel funny," she whispered. "Take them off."

Rick sat up abruptly and peeled off his shirt and shorts, then sat cross-legged while he absorbed the beauty of Amy's waiting body, his eyes lingering on her naked curves much as his camera had done. It was as though he were trying to record the image of her body onto his brain. Amy waited expectantly, for once comfortable with Rick's familiarity with her naked form. "I don't want you to ever think yourself less than perfect," he murmured as he ran his fingertips around her waist lightly. "Your breasts and hips are in perfect proportion, and your stomach and legs are absolutely divine. And your skin is like satin to touch," he murmured as he slid his hands up her stomach and over her breasts to her face, where he leaned down and kissed each cheek softly. He then reached down and planted a kiss into her navel, and smiled with satisfaction as her stomach muscles tensed in delicious anticipation. Amy felt a spasm of pleasure shoot through her body.

Slowly he lowered himself until he lay alongside her, drawing her to him and pushing the robe under her head for a pillow. Slowly, slowly, he kissed her mouth and her throat, lingering at her pulse points and teasing them with his tongue as fiery darts of pleasure shot through her body and shivers of delight spread down her spine. Rick lingered at her neck and caressed her face for timeless moments, seeming content to dwell there, and Amy grew impatient. But slowly she stilled the fiery impatience that threatened to consume her. Rick was teaching her a new way to make love, and she knew that if she followed his lead, she would experience a delight that would be beyond her wildest imagination. Imitating his tantalizing caresses, she slowly reached for him and covered his chest and throat with hot, wet kisses of her own.

Rick allowed his mouth to move lower, finding one small breast and rolling the small nipple between his tongue and teeth until he could feel it swell in his mouth. Involuntarily responding to his erotic touch, Amy dug her heels into the ground and arched upward, meeting his mouth with her body. His tongue wandered over to the other nipple, then captured it in his sensual hold. Amy squirmed in pleasure, feeling the jagged spikes of delight shoot through her breasts and down the rest of her body. "Oh, Rick," she moaned. "Rick!"

"Tell me, Amy . . . tell me what you want . . ." he murmured as he allowed his mouth to trail down her chest, returning to the erotic indentation in the middle of her stomach. He ran his tongue around the edge lightly, then plunged it into the center of her navel.

Amy's stomach muscles quivered as she grasped Rick's hair convulsively, making her unable to answer him. His mouth trailed back up her chest, but his hands remained warm on her stomach, caressing it with a gentle circular motion that was driving Amy wild.

Amy's hands crept down Rick's body until they found his hard bottom, where Amy found with her fingers the erotic dimples that she had noticed while they swam. Rick's hands continued to tantalize her body, doing delightful things to her hips and thighs, causing the shooting feelings of pleasure to travel up and down Amy's body and into her midsection. One hand strayed lower until it found her warm femininity. Gasping in surprise, Amy tensed for a moment, then relaxed as shyness gave way to pleasure. He probed and caressed her gently as Amy's expressive face mirrored her pleasure and her torment. His fingers tantalized Amy until she cried out in longing and frustration. "Don't wait any longer!" she moaned as she guided his hips to her own.

They made love with a ferocity that startled them both. Amy

150

met Rick's rhythm with a perfectly synchronized motion of her own. He threw himself into the lovemaking with savage abandon, and she met him with a sensual wildness that moved them both to the core of their beings. Their bodies were entangled in the beautiful sun-dappled shade, but they were unaware of their surroundings, so tuned were they to each other and the exquisite lovemaking that they shared. Amy could feel a mounting pressure building within her as their loving became more intense. Then upon reaching the ultimate of all of the sensations that had come before, she could feel waves of delight building in her midsection and spreading out to the extremities of her body. She murmured Rick's name as she felt the supreme satisfaction come to him, then they drifted down slowly, as did leaves falling in the wind.

Amy lay close to Rick, cradling his head between her breasts. He snuggled close to her and nuzzled her breasts with his nose and tongue. "I love the way you taste," he said softly. "And the way you look, the way you sound, and the way you feel." He sniffed appreciatively. "I even like the way you smell."

"Like fishy lake water?" Amy teased.

Rick laughed, but he looked at her seriously and kissed her between her breasts. "I just want you to know that I was profoundly moved by making love to you," he said softly. "It was like . . ." he trailed off uncertainly.

"I understand," Amy said softly. "It was like that for me, too." And it had been. Rick had indeed taught her a new way to make love, and she was still trembling in joy from the lesson. He had moved Amy profoundly, so much so that she could not put her feelings into words. She reached over and ran her hand down Rick's hairy chest. "You have a perfect body, you know," she said lovingly.

"No, I don't," Rick scoffed. "I'm too fat."

"You can't mean that!" Amy laughed. "You look great! It's me—I'm too thin."

"No, you're not," Rick objected. "You're just small." Together they surveyed their bodies lying together intimately, one large and muscular, the other small and soft. "The nice part of it is that they fit together so perfectly," he murmured as he rolled Amy over on her back and demonstrated again just how well they fit.

It was late when they arrived back at the cabin. Amy broiled a couple of steaks, promising Rick that she would demonstrate her culinary talents at a later date, and they ate their simple meal with relish, talking little but saying volumes with their eyes. After supper they walked along the beach again, letting the wind blow in their faces and ruffle their hair, and they watched the sun disappear behind a billowing thundercloud. "Looks like rain blowing in," Rick said thoughtfully.

"Oh, I hope so!" Amy said delightedly even as the first drops fell onto their faces. They ran back to the cabin just as the storm broke, sending sheets of rain into the lake and blowing the wetness onto the covered front porch, where Amy and Rick stood holding hands. "I just love a storm up here. It makes the lake so wild and beautiful!"

"I know something else that's wild and beautiful up here," Rick said as he swept her into his arms and carried her into the cabin, standing her by his bed and stripping the damp clothing from her body. Quickly he shed his own and then they stood naked, looking out at the wild, wonderful storm until Amy gently pushed Rick back onto the bed.

"You've made love to me twice today," she said as she covered his hard body with her own. "Now it's my turn." She covered his body with hers, maneuvering herself so that their bodies were locked together, her soft curves melting into his hard frame. She covered his face with light kisses, nibbling at his cheeks and chin, which were becoming rough with a day's growth of beard. "I love the way your beard feels," she said as she rubbed her cheek lightly against his chin.

"Don't scratch yourself on it," Rick said softly as he captured her face between his palms and kissed her sensuously, moving his tongue into the delightful warmth of her mouth. Amy raised up slightly and ran her lips down Rick's neck and chest, finding one of his nipples and tormenting it with her tongue, feeling as much pleasure in the giving as she would have in the taking.

Rick moaned and tried to sit up, but she would not let him. "No," she murmured. "I said that I would make love to you." And she did. She caressed every inch of Rick's delectable body, touching and exploring, with fingers tuned to his hard body and a willing mouth, all the intimate and hidden places until Rick was writhing in pleasure. She waited until he was almost wild with anticipation and stopped a minute.

"Don't stop now!" Rick muttered.

"I won't," Amy murmured, then returned to him and explored him again, driving herself almost crazy with pleasure in the process.

"I don't think I can take much more of this," Rick murmured as Amy ran her gentle fingers up his bare thigh.

"Neither can I!" Amy moaned as she slid back up onto his muscular body and covered it with her own. She moved over Rick and made love to him with all the fervor and excitement with which he had made love to her, arching herself above him when the storm of pleasure swept them both away in its frenzy.

The rest of the week was like a honeymoon. Rick insisted that they share a bed, but since there was no bed in the cabin that was big enough, they pushed together the daybeds and tied the legs together. They went on picnics every day, and visited every tourist trap in the vicinity. One day they toured Longhorn Caverns, natural caves hollowed out of limestone by years of water erosion. Another day they rode the paddle boats at Inks Lake, laughing when they startled the ducks. Rick tagged along cheerfully while Amy shopped at the various art galleries along the highway, and even bought one particularly good watercolor to

153

take home with him. And one evening they dressed in nicer clothes and ate out at a small restaurant overlooking the water. But the nights were best, because Rick would take Amy into his arms and make love to her, enslaving her body and her heart to him forever.

"I sure hate to go home," Rick said after they had made love the last night of their stay.

"So do I," Amy admitted. She looked up from Rick's shoulder and grinned impishly. "What if we just didn't go back? Let's just stay here and be beach bums!"

"That might satisfy you for one week. I'd last a week and a half. No, Amy, I'm afraid that we need more in our lives than just the simple life."

"I guess you're right," Amy acknowledged ruefully, thinking for the first time in days of the book she had yet to finish.

"When we get back we need to talk," Rick said slowly. "No, not here," he said as Amy turned to him questioningly. He reached down and kissed her, and passion flared between them again. "I'm going to make love to you again," he murmured. "If this week hasn't killed me, nothing will," he said as he pushed her into the pillows.

If anything, the week of shared intimacy had increased their desire for each other. Thoroughly familiar with each other's pleasure points, they kissed and caressed and enticed one another with abandon, each trying to give the other exquisite sensations. Amy rubbed Rick below his navel with her palm, and was rewarded with a groan of pleasure. He turned Amy over and reached around her, caressing her breasts and her stomach with his hands while he nibbled the back of her neck with his mouth. When they had reached a state of quivering readiness, Rick turned Amy back over and together they climbed to the nearest star, jumping off into the void of space together, and slowly settling back down to earth.

The sound of the telephone drew Amy from a sound and restful slumber. She felt Rick leave the bed and heard him swear as he picked up the telephone in the kitchen. She could not hear the conversation, but she heard Rick hang up the receiver and walk swiftly back into the main room. "Get up," he said tersely as he snapped on the light to augment the soft gray dawn. "We have to go back. Samantha just called. She needs me."

Amy sat up slowly. "We have to go back?" she asked in a dazed whisper.

"You heard me," Rick snapped as he pulled on a pair of jeans. "Now get a move on."

Amy stumbled to the bathroom. So Samantha had got word that they were up here. Amy's face crumpled and she sobbed quietly into her bath towel. She had thought this week that maybe Rick was learning to love her, that all of her dreams might come true. But one telephone call was all it took to summon Rick back to the woman he really loved. Resolutely Amy squared her shoulders and pulled on her clothes. Rick had just hurt her more than she ever thought she could be hurt, but she would be damned if she let him know. Throwing back her shoulders, she left the bathroom, ready for the long ride home.

CHAPTER NINE

Amy bent over and focused the microscope. "Can you see the organism right by the pointer?" she asked as Rick peered into the ocular.

"That oval-shaped thing with all the hairs?" Rick asked as he adjusted the focus.

"Cilia," Amy corrected automatically. "Yes, that's it. Can you get a picture of that?"

Rick removed a special camera from his case that was designed specifically for high magnification work, and screwed it into the top of the microscope. He looked into the viewer and cursed. "Damn it, I've lost the parasite. Get over here and locate it for me so I can get on with this."

Amy bit back a sarcastic retort and bent over the camera. She looked into the viewer and painstakingly relocated the organism, then motioned to Rick. "It's right beside the pointer. It's at a little different angle, but that's all right."

Rick nodded and set to work. He snapped three exposures and swore loudly. "The damned thing's moved again. Get over here and find it for me."

"Yes, sir!" Amy snapped, her patience gone. Rick's behavior

had been curt and rude all evening, and she had put up with all of his temper that she intended to tolerate. "Move over," she said as she elbowed her way in front of the microscope. She found the organism again and turned to Rick. "If you will try not to jiggle the microscope any more than you can help it—"

"You find the damned critter and I'll take the pictures!" Rick roared furiously.

"Then take your damned picture and shut your mouth!" Amy shot back. She stepped back angrily and let Rick have the scope.

Quickly, before the slide could slip again, he snapped five or six pictures and sighed in relief. "That does it," he said tiredly. Quickly he packed his camera bag and headed for the door. "I have to run. Samantha's waiting," he said as he left.

"Hooray for modern morals," Amy muttered bitterly as she brushed an unwanted tear from her eye. "He runs from one lover to the next and doesn't even try to hide it." But you knew that from the very beginning, she reminded herself as she cleaned up the lab. Did you really think that you would be any different from Linda or Samantha? "Yes, I did," she said out loud, appalled by her own gullibility. During their idyllic week on the lake Amy had pretended to herself that Rick loved her and that they had a future together, even though no words of love were ever spoken by either of them. She had a private fantasy of her and Rick sharing their lives together, loving and having children and growing old with one another. But the fantasy was shattered by one telephone call from Samantha.

Rick had rushed Amy to pack that morning in the cabin, and they left in such haste that they left the daybeds pushed together. Amy squirmed when she realized the interpretation that Dr. Thompson would put on that. Rick had hardly spoken on the drive back, and when she had tried to thank him for the week, he had cut her off abruptly and driven off, leaving Amy standing in the warm summer morning in front of her apartment with her suitcases and her dreams scattered at her feet.

Amy shrugged as she turned off the light to the laboratory and

157

left. At least they had got the pictures that she needed tonight, and since this was her last week to work for Patterson's Pics, she would not have to be around Rick anymore and be constantly reminded of her foolishness.

Actually, tonight was the first time that Amy had seen anything of Rick since he had dropped her at her apartment almost a week ago. He had not been at the studio at the same times that Amy was there, and Betty Jean let it slip that Joe and Tommy Lee were still covering most of Rick's assignments. Amy wondered waspishly if he had taken Samantha away on a vacation also. However, he apparently had remembered that they had arranged to finish her pictures tonight, and he showed up to do that.

As Amy drove past the street that led to Samantha's apartment she gave in to a petty impulse and drove by the highrise slowly, looking for Rick's car or a light in Samantha's window. She saw neither, but Samantha's Porsche was parked in its designated space. But that didn't mean anything, she told herself. They might be out on the town, or at a friend's house, or even alone at Rick's place. Angrily Amy blocked out the images that sprang into her mind of Samantha in Rick's big bed, of Rick's muscular body covering Samantha's, of Samantha's lips on his. Resolutely Amy vowed to forget the treacherous photographer who had broken her heart.

She typed late into the night, feverishly refining her text until it was the superb script that she had known she was capable of turning out. Rick had accomplished his goal by kidnapping her, she thought bitterly. In spite of the anguish she felt by his betrayal, her body at least was rested and she could once more produce the kind of work that had got her where she was today in the academic world.

Sighing, Amy poured herself her usual glass of milk and stared out the window of her living room at the sparse traffic. Would I have had a chance if Rick had not been involved with Samantha? No, she told herself sadly, you wouldn't have. You just couldn't have kept him satisfied for long, and you know it. Unbidden, thoughts of their lovemaking sprang to Amy's mind, and she relived the touch of Rick's body intimately entwined with hers on the blanket under the leaves, then remembered the feel of Rick's hard arm thrown across her waist in the cozy cocoon of the daybeds. Groaning, she wrenched her thoughts from the intimate moments of their affair. She could not torture herself with those thoughts, or she would go crazy. Amy swallowed the last of the milk and twisted her ring absently. And could Rick have satisfied me? she wondered. She refused herself the luxury of speculating on the answer to that one, since she would never have the chance to find out.

Amy parked her car and walked into Patterson's Pics for the last time as an employee of the establishment. She would start the new fall semester and her duties as an associate professor on Monday, and this Friday was her last day at Patterson's. Amy realized with a pang that she would miss the place horribly. Not just Rick, but Betty Jean and Tommy Lee and even the irrepressible Joe. She supposed that she could come and visit, but she would miss the sincere acceptance these people had given to her, and the plain old fun she had experienced doing something new and different from her usual grind. She bit her lip as unwanted tears blurred her eyes. Way down deep, she knew that she would not come back for a long time, even for a visit. It would hurt too much to see Rick.

Betty Jean seemed preoccupied as she handed Amy a set of checks from customers to enter into the computer's bookkeeping system. Amy seized the chance to work by herself and not have to talk to anyone. Tommy Lee banged in and out as usual, but Rick was nowhere to be seen. Joe was holed up in the studio, working on a difficult assignment, and had issued strict orders that he was not to be disturbed.

The afternoon sped by. The billing had taken only a few minutes to finish, but Betty Jean asked Amy to transfer as many of the records for the past two years as she could into a program to show the IRS if it became necessary, and Amy worked swiftly to complete the job if she could. Joe and Tommy Lee wandered back in and found some copy work waiting for them, and with some good-natured grumbling fell to the task. As the clock moved closer to five Betty Jean slipped into the studio and closed the door behind her.

Amy finished the program and filed it on a disk, then sighed and turned off the computer. She would have to tell everyone good-bye now, and she hated to. She looked around, but everyone had disappeared into the studio in direct violation of Joe's orders. Tentatively she knocked on the door, and was greeted with a gruff "Come in." She did so gingerly and was astonished by a chorus of "Surprise!" Amy looked up and gasped in astonishment. They were giving her a party!

Suddenly Amy realized that she had finally arrived as a person. Somehow, she had been accepted by this diverse, wonderful group of people as one of them. And she knew that she had Rick to thank for that. It was because of his acceptance of her that she had allowed the others to accept her, too. Finally she had broken out of her intellectual mold and had begun to relate to the rest of humanity as a fellow human being. She was just like everybody else! She was warm, she was sensual, she was loved and loving. And she owed the miracle to Rick. If he had not shown her this new, exciting dimension to her nature, she might have never known what she had missed all this time. In spite of the pain that Rick had inflicted on her soul, she knew that she owed him for this.

Laughing and crying at the same time, Amy hugged and kissed Betty Jean and the photographers who had secretly assembled this grand sendoff. A lot of their regular customers and models were there. They had sneaked in the back door while Amy worked in the front office. A cup of beer was thrust into her hand, and she spotted a table laden with nachos, tamales, and other casual hors d'oeuvres. Amy led the way to the table and loaded a plate with food, and soon everyone in the room was eating and talking merrily. Joe ribbed Amy unmercifully about her now legendary mastery of the computer in one afternoon, and Betty Jean complained that now she would have to learn to use the computer herself.

A hush fell briefly over the room, and then shouts of "It's about time" and "Come on in" filled the room as Rick came in the door. He looked tired and as though he had lost weight, but he was smiling broadly.

"Is everything all right?" Betty Jean asked anxiously.

Rick smiled broadly as he winked impudently at Amy. "Yes, Betty Jean," he said. "It's going to be all right." He turned to Amy and handed her an envelope. "It's from Samantha," he said. "It's a gift certificate for Small Ladies, Please, her new boutique."

So you think it's going to be all right, Amy thought waspishly. You soothed Samantha's ruffled feathers or solved whatever her problem was, and you think you can come running back to me. Oh, no, buddy, Amy thought angrily. You have another think coming. Maybe Rick saw nothing distasteful about multiple bed partners, she reminded herself. Some people didn't. Hurt suddenly replaced anger in Amy's mind, and as Rick wandered over to the table of food it was all Amy could do to keep from bursting into tears. Why did she have to fall so hard for someone whose attitudes and values were so different from her own, a man who would never be content with just her? They came from different worlds, she and Rick.

Amy got another cup of beer and mingled with the crowd. Her pleasure in the party was gone, but she did not want Betty Jean or the men who had worked so hard to please her to know. She spoke to everyone, and heard over and over again how much her help had been appreciated and how much she would be missed. The kind words meant much to her, since she had been a novice around anything photographic. Tommy Lee made a special point of thanking her and wishing her well, and she wondered what the talented teenager would be doing in ten years.

The party finally began to thin out as one by one the guests took their leave. As Amy began helping Betty Jean clear the table Rick slipped up behind Amy and put his arm around her shoulders. She stiffened and tried to pull away without being obvious about it, but Rick tightened his grip and pulled her close to his side. "Why are you drawing away, pretty lady?" he whispered in her ear as he gave her a look that was warm and tender.

"This is a bit public," Amy said softly, not willing to provoke a confrontation here. She would say what she had to in private.

"I'll be over this evening," Rick said softly. "I'll bring a bottle of wine, and we'll celebrate."

What will we celebrate? Amy wondered silently. Your virility? She shook her head, suddenly tired and not willing to talk to him tonight. "Not tonight, Rick," she said quietly.

"Why not?" he demanded imperiously. "It's been a week since I've seen you."

"I'm busy!" Amy snapped sharply. Rick looked at her suspiciously and dropped his arm from her shoulders. Joe chose that moment to make his farewells to Amy, and by the time he had moved on, Betty Jean had called Rick to the telephone. He shot Amy a hard look as he strode rapidly into his office.

Amy hugged Betty Jean and the men, promising to come and visit when she could, and left Patterson's for the last time. She drove around aimlessly for an hour or so, not wanting to return to her empty apartment and wait for Monday to come. Finally, as her gas gauge dipped precariously low, she headed back to her apartment.

She slipped out of her clothes and ran the shower as hot as she could stand it, then let the pounding spray beat into her skin until she had relaxed for the first time in a week. She dried herself and wrapped herself in the terry robe, then sat down and flipped on the television while she dried her wet hair with a towel. She

162

heard a car pull up in front of the apartment but, assuming it was one of her neighbors, did not look out the window.

She jumped when the three heavy knocks shook her front door. It had to be Rick. Amy took a deep breath. It would do no good to ignore the pounding. Rick was perfectly capable of standing out on the steps and pounding the door all night, if that was what it took. Her composure gone, Amy snapped off the safety chain and opened the door a crack. Rick pushed the door open and strode in, an exasperated expression on his face.

"Why did you say you were busy?" he asked impatiently.

"I was," Amy returned calmly, not allowing her inner anguish to show in her face. "I was drying my hair and watching the television."

"Don't be ridiculous," Rick replied. "You knew that I wanted to see you and that this is the first chance I've had all week to do that. Come here, woman, I want to kiss you." He started over to her but stopped, frozen in midstep by the look on her face.

"Sit down, Rick," she said quietly. "I have to talk to you."

Rick sat down in the armchair and looked at Amy. "Say what you have to say," he said coldly.

Amy took a deep breath and expelled it slowly. "I will always treasure the memory of the week we spent together at the lake," she said, tension threading her voice at the thought of what she was about to do.

Rick nodded. "So will I," he said softly.

"But I think we shouldn't see each other anymore," Amy choked out. The hateful words would barely come out of her mouth.

"Do go on," he said, his voice dangerously quiet. "I'm not going to help you."

"What we had up there was a moment out of time, something special. But in our everyday lives things are different. You understand." Amy bit her lip. This was much harder than she had imagined that it would be.

"As a matter of fact, I don't," Rick said softly, his voice menacing. "Enlighten me."

"We come from—two different worlds," she stammered in anguish. "You do some things differently in yours than I do in mine. I don't think that we would get along very well once we started trying to cope with things here, so I don't think we should spoil our memories of a beautiful time." Amy cringed, knowing that she sounded hard and cold. If Rick only knew the pain she was suffering!

Rick looked at her angrily and lit a cigarette. "That's a bunch of garbage and you know it," he snarled as he looked her in the eye. "We got along beautifully up there, and we've got along just great most of the time down here." He looked at her shrewdly. "You're going to have to do better than that."

"I don't have to do anything at all," Amy retorted with spirit, her anguish momentarily replaced by anger. "I have asked that we not see one another anymore, and I've tried to explain to you why. I think that's all I should have to say." She gritted her teeth. Should she tell him exactly why she would not see him again?

No, she said to herself. I just can't. It would be all too easy for him to lie about the past week, and dummy that I am, I'd fall for it. And then I will end up getting hurt much worse later. No, I'll keep on with this farce. I've been hurt enough already.

"I think you owe me, Amy," Rick said through gritted teeth. "You know the way it was between us. You're throwing it away, and I don't know why."

"If you will think about it, I bet you'll be able to figure it out," Amy snapped.

Rick looked at her. "You say that we are too different, that we don't have something important in common. What? I just can't see it. I simply can't see what trivial little issue is bothering you."

Did he really consider his involvement with Samantha trivial? Was he so without morals that he couldn't see what that would

164

do to her? Incredulous, she shook her head. "Are you so dense that you can't tell what's bothering me?"

Rick's face hardened into stone. "So that's it," he snarled. "We're back to that damned intellect of yours."

"That isn't what I meant," Amy said as she caught her breath in surprise. She had never thought that Rick would put that interpretation on her actions.

"Oh, sure it is," Rick bit out, his face contorted with pained rage. "Only you're too genteel to come out and say, 'Rick, you're too dumb for the fancy atmosphere that I breathe, too stupid to spend my time with.' "

"That's not true," Amy cried. Rick really believed that was why she did not want to see him anymore!

"I'm disappointed in you, Amy," he continued angrily. "I honestly thought you were above the petty snobbery that so many of your brilliant buddies indulge in, but in the crunch, you're just like them. You think you're better than everybody else. All that about wanting to be accepted by ordinary men was a bunch of hogwash. When an ordinary man does express an interest in you, you cut him off like a faucet."

"You're twisting things to suit your own interpretation," Amy spat at him, her tormented anguish giving way to an anger that matched Rick's. "You aren't willing to admit to what the problem really is, so you fall back on the first stupid thing you can think of, which happens to be wrong."

"Oh, I'm not wrong," Rick said bitterly. If she had not known better, she would have thought there were tears in his eyes. "I've met too many like you before. Well, you can keep your attentions for someone whose intellect you can approve of, and you can talk about all the fancy scientific theories you want to in your bed while I go and find me a real woman to share mine."

"I thought you already had two or three of those," Amy taunted spitefully.

"Yes, I have," Rick said as he jerked open the front door, "and

I may have a few more before I'm through. And most of them could teach you a thing or two about it!"

Amy stood dry-eyed and silent as she watched Rick drive away. She had just sent away the love of her life, and she felt that she had just torn her heart out and sent it with him. Numb with shock, she realized now that the emotion she had felt for Miles had been nothing compared to the love she felt for Rick, yet this time the break had been of her own choosing and she shed no tears. He was not worth crying over. Amy reached up and pounded the wall with her fist, swearing at the irony. Rick was one of the few men who could have accepted her intellect, and she could not accept his life-style.

Damn it, why couldn't I have taken whatever he had to offer? Plenty of other women would have, and been glad to get it! Am I too prim, too demanding? What if I went to him? I know he would forget the fight. He's very forgiving. But then he would expect me to be forgiving too, and forgive him Samantha and Linda and all of the others. "And that's the crunch," Amy said out loud. "I couldn't forgive him for that." And she knew that if she made Rick a part of her life, she would have to forgive him often.

"Damn," Amy shouted at the empty walls of her apartment as at last tears began to fall. "There's no way. Damn it to hell!" she screamed at the top of her lungs. "There isn't any way."

Amy assumed her new role as associate professor with a vengeance. She was teaching three different courses now, in addition to new administrative duties that kept her in her office late into the evening. Her classes were full, and the bright young students kept Amy running to the library to search out the answers to their more astute questions. Her publisher asked for several rewrites, which filled Amy's days even further. She smiled and she laughed and she thrived on the new responsibilities. And if her smile was a bit strained and her laughter a bit shrill, no one seemed to notice. She felt her appetite falling off and attributed it to her busy schedule and not to any other reason. She resolutely pushed thoughts of Rick from her mind during her waking hours, and if she sometimes woke in the morning with a pillow damp with tears, she chalked it up to bitter experience. She searched the want ads for a cat, but never bothered to call any of the numbers.

As the months passed Amy grew philosophical. Although the tormenting pain of losing Rick was always with her, she consoled herself with the new research project that she had in its preliminary stages. David was dating one of the graduate students in sociology, and she wished him well. But if it was not meant for her to be with the man she loved so dearly, then it would not be. She would continue to cope with the pain and the loneliness as best she could. Armed with that philosophy, she returned to her job and her life, although she acknowledged to herself that there was something missing in the center of it.

CHAPTER TEN

"This press party is quite an honor," Dr. Thompson said as he set his coffee mug back on his desk.

"I know," Amy murmured, swallowing the last of her coffee and pouring another cup. "I didn't realize that the book would warrant that," she said. "Especially since it won't be out for months yet."

Dr. Thompson twisted his swivel chair around and gazed out the window at the chill campus, the blustering winds of the first norther of the season swaying the branches and blowing the leaves off the trees. "The university is trying to push its involvement in local and regional conservation efforts," he said cynically. "The tremendous environmental impact that your mussel medicine will have on the natural fauna of the region will give the university a lot of free PR."

"Unless someone starts screaming about dumping chemicals in the rivers and lakes," Amy said impishly. "I hope the press understands that the substance is biodegradable."

"That's your job to explain," Dr. Thompson said. "After all, you developed the medicine, you wrote the book, and you'll be making all those royalties . . ."

"Cute!" Amy teased back. "When and where do I show up?"

"It will be the Tuesday before Thanksgiving," he replied. "You will field questions from the press, and Rick can have a turn explaining the technical aspects of his outstanding photography."

"Rick's going to be there?" Amy asked quietly.

Dr. Thompson looked at her shrewdly. He had not forgot those daybeds. "He'll be invited to speak on his contribution to the book."

"Of course," Amy stammered, her heart pounding, the memory she had tried to wipe out rushing back to haunt her. Would she have the strength to face him after nearly three months?

She would have to, whether or not she felt that she could. She would have had to sooner or later. Betty Jean had called her twice and asked her to come by the studio for a visit, and if she did not get down there soon, she was going to hurt Betty Jean's feelings. She had built an armor of sorts around herself in the last three months, and now she was going to have to try that armor out.

"Should I contact him myself?" Amy asked. "Or will the committee do it for me?"

"I'm sure he will receive a letter from the committee," Dr. Thompson said. "But I feel that a personal note from you would be a gracious touch."

"Will do," Amy said. She finished her coffee and set her mug on the desk. "I better get going," she said. Dr. Thompson watched her go, a frown of concern on his face for the too-thin young woman who never smiled with her eyes anymore.

That evening Amy sat at her desk and penned a short note to Rick. She tore up her first two attempts and threw them into the trash, but finally settled on a simple paragraph informing Rick that the press party would be on the Tuesday before Thanksgiving at the Hilton Hotel, and that the university would like for him to speak briefly about his part in the project. She added that she looked forward to his contribution to the evening and signed it simply "Amy." As she mailed the letter the next morning she thought that maybe it was a good thing that she was being forced to face Rick. Maybe by seeing him again she could exorcise the ghost of him that haunted her days and disturbed her dreams. The more Amy thought about it, the more convinced she became that seeing Rick again would be a good thing.

Dr. Thompson had made it clear that Amy would be the recipient of most of the press's attention, and on the day before the press party she vowed that, at least for one night, she would not look like the old maid schoolteacher that Rick had once teased her about being. Since she felt that most of her clothes placed her in that category, she planned a shopping trip to remedy the situation. Checking the balance in her checkbook, she remembered the gift certificate that sat in the bottom of her desk drawer to Small Ladies, Please, and drew it out of the drawer. Why not? she thought. She had sincerely liked Samantha, and the certificate would go a long way toward a new outfit for the occasion. Resolutely Amy placed the certificate in her wallet and headed for Small Ladies, Please.

Located right next door to Samantha's other boutique, the shop was a wonderland for a small woman like Amy. There was a plentiful selection of business suits and dresses, evening wear, and sportswear, all designed and made with the smaller woman in mind. Amy looked through more clothes in her size than she had ever seen assembled in one place, and finally chose a bright peach suit and print blouse that did great things for her thin figure and her now-pale skin, although even in her small size the suit was a bit too loose. The saleswoman volunteered to have the waist taken up a bit while Amy waited. While the tailor quickly made the alterations Amy wandered around, examining the selection of clothing and accessories. She did not recognize any of the saleswomen from the other store, but she assumed that Samantha had hired all new people for the new boutique.

The saleswoman returned with the altered suit, and Amy brought out her checkbook and the gift certificate. The woman examined the certificate for a moment, then said, "Excuse me," and went into the office.

In a moment a friendly young woman came out and read the certificate. "It was signed by Samantha Westermann, so we can honor it with no problem," she told the saleswoman as she turned to go back to the office.

"Excuse me," Amy said to the retreating woman. "Doesn't Samantha own this shop?"

"No, she set about half of it up and then sold it to us, and my partners and I finished the ordering and opened it."

Why had Samantha sold her new shop? Amy wondered about that all the way home. Samantha had seemed so excited about it that day at her apartment. Did she decide to reduce her demanding business schedule so that she could spend more time with Rick? Amy shook her head. That did not sound like Samantha at all. No, there had to be another reason. Amy wondered about it a little longer, then started working on her notes for the press party and forgot all about Samantha.

The evening of the press party turned cold and rainy. Amy appreciated the warmth of her new suit and her fashionable gray coat as she walked from the parking garage to the downtown hotel. She walked up the steps into the busy lobby and followed the signs to the elevator that would carry her to the next floor, where the press party was to be held. Dr. Thompson had arrived already and was standing beside the president of the university, who greeted Amy cordially and commented that her research had done much to improve the university's image in the community's eyes. Amy caught Dr. Thompson's eye and tried not to laugh. She helped herself to a few hors d'oeurves and a glass of water, then chatted with the press as she surreptitiously watched the door for some sign of Rick. She had not heard from him, but then she had not expected to. She assumed that he would understand the importance of this evening to his career as well as her own.

Finally, as the reporters began to sit down in the chairs arranged in front of a table and lectern, Amy approached Dr. Thompson and gestured with her arm toward the door. "Where's Rick? He's supposed to be here."

"He's not coming," Dr. Thompson said quietly. "He had something else that he had to do."

"Damn his hide!" Amy snapped. She felt completely humiliated. Rick knew how important this evening was to her and to his own career yet he had found something better to do. She turned to Dr. Thompson with anger and hurt mingled on her face. "So what do I do?" she said.

"First, you calm down," Dr. Thompson commanded quietly. "It isn't what you think. Then, you answer all the questions that are asked to the best of your ability, and if you can't answer a question that was intended for Rick, you say so. After this is over with, wait for me. I'll take you out for a drink."

He must want to talk to me about something, Amy thought. He'd never in his life gone out for a drink that she knew of. She took her place at the table and tuned out the introductions that droned from the university brass. Why hadn't Rick come tonight? Was he still so angry that he preferred to ignore her altogether? Amy thought about their last painful meeting. Had she hurt him that much?

The sound of her own name snapped Amy out of her reverie, and she listened to the introduction, then took her place behind the podium. She had spent many hours before classes that were more critical and less friendly than these reporters, and she looked and felt completely at ease. She gave a brief synopsis of her work and her results, then offered to answer any and all of the questions that she could, explaining that Rick Patterson, the photographer on the project, was unable to attend.

They fired questions at her for an hour, but she was more than able to answer them. She was even able to respond to a few of the questions regarding Rick's work, and the reporters were unusually gracious about the ones that she could not answer. She

172

promised them another interview when the book came out, and teasingly made them promise that they would all buy the book and read it. As the university publicity officer made his closing remarks she wondered how she could refuse Dr. Thompson graciously and go home, to face alone her disappointment at not seeing Rick tonight. She was angry that he had not come, but when she examined her feelings she realized that she was equally disappointed. She had looked forward to seeing him again.

Dr. Thompson found her slipping on her coat. "Are you ready for that drink?" he asked as he struggled into his overcoat.

"I guess so," Amy replied less than enthusiastically.

Dr. Thompson ignored her reluctance and escorted her out of the banquet hall. "I know a nice spot here on the river that isn't too noisy," he said as he led the way out the back doors of the Hilton and onto the Riverwalk. They walked in silence along the sidewalk, fighting the wind that blew in their faces. The river was almost deserted, and the few people who were there were hurrying to get inside the taverns or restaurants that were open. They walked around a curve and entered a small, smoky bar that was homey and quiet. Dr. Thompson led Amy to a table in the corner and asked the waitress for two glasses of wine. While the waitress was bringing the wine Dr. Thompson talked about how well Amy had gone over with the press and how, if she wasn't careful, she would end up a media star. Amy smiled and nodded and waited for Dr. Thompson to get to the point.

The waitress returned with their wine. Dr. Thompson took a sip and nodded. "This is good wine for a place like this," he said. "So what happened between you and Rick?"

"Nothing like jumping right into it," Amy said wryly. "Why wasn't he there tonight? He knew how important it was to me!"

"He had something he had to do today," Dr. Thompson said. "His old friend Samantha Westermann—"

"Yes, I should have known," Amy said bitterly. "Samantha needed him."

"Yes, she did. She's needed him for months, but after today

173

he won't be seeing her for a while," Dr. Thompson said tiredly. "Rick took Samantha to Houston and checked her into a rehabilitation and therapy center there."

Amy's glass slid through her fingers and hit the table with a thump, splashing wine all over the tablecloth. "What happened to her?" she asked through stiff lips.

"Samantha was in a nasty car accident back in August," Dr. Thompson said. "She was in a coma for nearly a week, and she suffered severe brain damage. Only in the last few weeks has she responded enough to begin further rehabilitation."

Guilty tears stung Amy's eyes. So that explained Rick's sudden departure from the lake, and his preoccupation the following week. "I'm sorry," Amy said quietly as she sipped her wine. "She's a lovely person and didn't deserve that. So Rick really couldn't be there tonight."

"He was going to try to make it, but I told him not to," Dr. Thompson said firmly. "He's been through the last months with her, and then would have had to rush back from Houston. He's just about at the end of his rope."

In spite of everything, compassion poured out of Amy. "I'm sorry for him," she said. "I wish it hadn't happened to her."

"Amy, I'm going to ask you again. What happened between you and Rick? And don't say nothing. The daybeds didn't get that way by themselves."

"I can't talk about it," Amy replied with a tremor in her voice. "It's still too painful."

"I don't think you're the only one who was hurt by that episode," Dr. Thompson said flatly. "Rick hasn't been the same since summer. Something inside of him died."

Amy snorted. "Well, it wasn't because of me!" she snapped. Then she remembered. "I'm sure that Rick was upset about Samantha," she said softly. "He loves her very much." Amy shrugged. "All I did was dent his pride."

"How did you do that?" Dr. Thompson probed gently.

"I told him that it would never work between us. I broke our affair off, rather abruptly, I admit, but I gave him a reason, and it isn't my fault that he wouldn't accept it." The pain in Amy's eyes belied the firmness of her voice, and her usual jabbing forefinger fluttered helplessly.

"What reason did you give him?" Dr. Thompson asked as he finished his wine.

"The truth. That we come from two completely different worlds and that it could never work between us."

Dr. Thompson looked as hard as Amy had ever seen him. "I didn't realize that you were an intellectual snob, Amy," he said coldly.

"That's what Rick accused me of being," Amy said furiously as she banged the wineglass down on the table, further splattering the tablecloth. "And you're both wrong, dead wrong! I happen to find Rick an extremely intelligent, stimulating individual!"

"Then what's all this nonsense about 'different worlds'? You were good together, weren't you?"

"The best," Amy admitted unashamedly, not referring entirely to the sexual side of their relationship. "At least it was for me. For Rick, I don't know, and I don't especially want to." His parting words had hurt her more than she cared to admit. "Look, Dr. Thompson, I'm the kind of woman who wants a home and a family, even though those are a little out of date these days. That's why I wanted to marry David even though he didn't light any fires for me. David offered me that. With Rick I had the sparks and the fire, but then so did two other women that I know of. I'm just not made like that. Rick loved Samantha Westermann, but even she couldn't hold him, as beautiful and lovely as she was. What chance would I have? I'm just a prim scholar."

Dr. Thompson looked quite disturbed. "Of course I don't know, but I seriously doubt that Rick would sleep with two women at once. That just doesn't sound like the Rick I know."

"But after that beautiful week we spent at the lake he practically ran me home so he could go to Samantha." Even now the hurt quivered in Amy's voice.

"And you didn't even ask Rick for an explanation?" Dr. Thompson asked incredulously.

Amy shook her head miserably. "I thought he would come up with a good lie and I'd just be hurt worse later," she said. "I guess he left because Samantha was hurt, but it doesn't make any difference now, anyway. I told you, there's no way that I could hold a vital, sensuous man like Rick."

"Oh, Amy, you're so wrong!" Dr. Thompson's eyes were filled with sympathy. "If you gave him a chance to love you, he would be more than satisfied. My love taught me that."

"But you and Edna had much more in common than Rick and I do," Amy protested. "When the passion wore out you had something else going for you."

Dr. Thompson shook his head slowly. "I wasn't talking about Edna," he said softly. "The love of my life was Marianne."

"You were married before?" Amy asked quietly.

Dr. Thompson nodded. "She was an artist. She had very little formal education, but she was a genius with a brush. I was a homely young scholar with two left feet and no money to boot. We fell in love."

"She was—how can I say it?—warm, loving, earthy, sensual. She scared me to death. I didn't think I would ever keep her happy, so I tried to break off our affair. Yes, even back then we had affairs," he said, noting Amy's look of surprise. "Marianne wouldn't let me. She convinced me that I was all she would ever need and, miraculously, I was. We spent thirty years together. After a few years we learned to ignore the intellectual snobbery around the university, and we were very happy."

"You're saying that you think we had a chance," Amy said. "And I blew it."

"Not just you," Dr. Thompson said. "I'm surprised that Rick gave up so easily. Unless Samantha's illness absorbed all of his time."

"Or I was just a diversion," Amy added. "I'll never know, now."

Dr. Thompson eyed her thoughtfully. "I'm going to meddle again," he said. "I'm getting quite good at it as far as you're concerned. I think you should go to Rick. Even if I'm wrong about him loving you, he needs someone very badly right now."

"I couldn't do that," Amy objected quickly, darting a look at her drink. She wanted to finish this conversation and get away from Dr. Thompson and his bright idea as quickly as she could, although another part of her acknowledged that it would be the kind thing to do.

"Why not?" Dr. Thompson asked firmly. "He helped you when you needed it."

"Sure," Amy gibed sarcastically. "What am I supposed to say to him? That you've sent me on a mission of mercy? Damn," she continued angrily. "I'm just not going."

"Amy, I never knew that you were a chicken," Dr. Thompson taunted. "Look, I'm not asking you to make a lifetime commitment, for God's sake. Just go and make sure that the man's all right."

Amy sighed tiredly. "All right. Is he at his apartment?"

Dr. Thompson valiantly stifled the twinkle in his eye. "He asked me if he could use the lake house for a few days. I think you'll find him there."

Amy rubbed her tired eyes and stared into the blowing storm. The rain fell in sheets across the highway, cutting visibility to a minimum, and the howling wind battered her Nova unmercifully. Still, she felt that she had to go to Rick now. If she waited until morning, she would talk herself out of it and might never have the chance to repay Rick's kindnesses to her. Swearing softly at the weather, she rounded a curve in the highway and looked out over Lake LBJ. The water was rough and choppy on this small lake, and Amy knew that it would be far worse on

Buchanan Lake. It seemed colder up here than it had in San Antonio, but that might be her own fear and loneliness.

What kind of reception would she get from Rick? She hardly expected warmth, not after their last meeting. She hoped he would be calm and let her look after him for a few days, and not coldly turn her away at the door. He might prefer to be alone to recover from the strain of almost losing Samantha, in which case her presence would be an unwelcome intrusion. Yet, she was glad that she had let Dr. Thompson persuade her to go to Rick. If nothing else, she could see him again and make sure that he was all right. She harbored no false hopes for a reconciliation, in spite of Dr. Thompson's revelations about his first wife. She just wanted to help Rick if she could.

The damp cold penetrated Amy's jeans and sweater in spite of the heater. She had taken off her good suit and thrown a few pairs of jeans and some tops in a suitcase. Since her only boots were already at the cabin, she had on a pair of tennis shoes that were doing very little to keep her feet warm. But it was just a few more miles and then she could be warm, unless Rick turned her away at the door.

The cabin was dark. Amy wondered briefly if Rick had not come up after all, then she saw the Datsun parked in back of the house and realized that it was after midnight and Rick had probably already gone to bed. She got her suitcase out of the trunk and pushed gently on the front door. It slid open, and Amy walked into the cold, clammy cabin. She felt her way to the kitchen and switched on the light, then peered into the dimly lit main room.

The table was covered with photographs sorted into neat piles, and an open album sat to one side of the pictures. An empty Scotch bottle and a full ashtray sat on top of the coffee table, and Rick's inert form was sprawled across the daybed that Amy usually occupied. Amy tiptoed over to Rick and bent over him. As she had expected, the odor of Scotch tinged his breath and his breathing was heavy. He was still dressed in a gray suit, but

178

his tie was loosened and the vest unbuttoned. Amy shook his arm gently.

"Rick, it's Amy," she said softly.

There was no response. Amy tried again. "Rick, can you hear me?" she asked, louder this time. Rick snored softly. "Oh, boy. He's out like a light."

She managed with much struggling to remove his coat and tie, and found a blanket to cover him with. In the dim light she could see that he looked exhausted and had lines of strain running from his nose to his mouth. His eyes had deep circles around them, and she could pick out a few gray hairs at his temples. She spread the blanket over his inert form and kissed him gently on the mouth. "I love you," she murmured.

Since the firewood was wet, she dragged an electric space heater out of the closet and plugged it in between the daybeds. Its coils gave off enough light so that Amy could move around the cabin freely. She unpacked the food that she brought, and found a blanket for the other daybed. She hesitated to look at Rick's pictures for fear of invading his privacy, but realized that she would have to move them in the morning anyway, so she shut the album and moved it. Then she picked up the first stack of pictures. She looked down at the photographs in her hand, then gasped as a shaft of pain tore through her body at the site of them, and she stifled an urge to throw the pictures out in the rain and leave the cabin. Quickly she riffled through the pictures that she held, then examined the stacks of photographs on the table. Every one of them was of Samantha.

The pictures were grouped by date, the oldest being of Samantha in college, and more recent ones in the other piles of approximately five-year time spans. Mesmerized, Amy looked at the pictures in chronological order. Samantha a college coed, climbing a jungle gym in the park, eating a Sno-Kone at the carnival. College graduation. Pictures of Samantha on a trip somewhere in Europe. An older, more beautiful Samantha behind an office desk, enjoying a party, standing arm in arm with Rick at the opening of Patterson's Pics. Samantha at the opening of her first boutique. A very recent picture of Samantha standing in front of what was to become Small Ladies, Please.

Controlling her urge to destroy the pictures, Amy laid them down carefully and stared out the window at the pouring rain. If ever she needed proof, now she had it. Samantha was indeed the woman whom Rick loved, in spite of his promiscuity. She, Amy, could never hope to win Rick's love. She quelled her intense feelings of jealousy for the hapless Samantha and forced herself to deal with her feelings of rejection logically. Rick had never asked her for her love, nor had he ever offered her his. Samantha was the love of his life, and she, Amy, was a friend and sometimes a lover but nothing more. So now what should she do? Amy looked long and lovingly at the man asleep on the daybed. She would be that friend to him, if that's all he needed her to be. And tomorrow, if he did not want her to stay, she would go and understand, although it would kill her.

Amy woke early the next morning, in spite of the late hour that she had finally gone to bed. Rick was still asleep, but the heater had done its work and the cabin was relatively warm. Amy showered and dressed as quickly as she could, and started a percolator of coffee brewing. She opened a package of bacon and put most of it into the pan, then popped four pieces of bread into the toaster. When they were done she set two places at the table and sat down with her breakfast.

She heard Rick rustling around on his daybed. "What is that Godawful smell?" he grumbled as he threw back the blanket.

"Breakfast," Amy said calmly, not showing her inner fear at the reception she was about to get.

Rick walked across the room and tilted her chin up to his gaze. "It really is you," he said quietly. "I thought I was dreaming." He fumbled through his suitcase and found a pair of jeans and a pullover top, then stumbled toward the bathroom, holding his head in his hands.

Amy had poured him a cup of coffee and put two dry pieces

of toast on his plate by the time he came out of the shower. He drank a few sips of the coffee and nibbled the toast while Amy watched him through her lashes. He didn't seem hostile or unfriendly, just indifferent. He finished one piece of the toast and poured himself another cup of coffee.

"Would you like a piece of bacon?" Amy asked.

"God, no," he muttered. He sat at the table while Amy cleared away the dishes and put away the blankets. Finally he looked around the room. "Where are all the pictures?" he asked.

"Over here," Amy said quickly as she handed Rick the album. He shook his head, and Amy put it away again. "I heard about Samantha," she said tentatively. "I'm sorry she was hurt so badly."

"So am I," Rick said abruptly. He pushed his chair back and picked up an overcoat. "I'm going for a walk. It might help this hangover."

Amy watched out the window as Rick walked down the curve of the beach, turning back to the room only when he disappeared around the bend. She curled up in the big chair and watched the waves pound the beach. The rain had stopped, but the sky was overcast and huge whitecaps disturbed the surface of the water. Had she made a big mistake in coming here? Should she go before Rick came back? No, if she did that, she would be able to do nothing to help him recover from his ordeal with Samantha, and she wanted to help him if she could. It was the least she could do for the man she loved.

Rick did not return to the cabin until lunchtime. Amy had found dry wood and started a fire in the fireplace, and she had prepared a hearty stew for their meal. Rick ate an adequate serving, although he lacked his usual lusty appetite. Amy picked at her stew listlessly.

"It's no wonder you've got so damned skinny, if that's all you've been eating lately," Rick said suddenly.

"I don't have much time to eat," Amy said levelly. "The new job is keeping me pretty busy."

"How's it going?" Rick asked dully.

Amy shrugged. "It's there," she said.

"Is it what you wanted?" Rick asked.

"It's very challenging and I enjoy it very much," she replied. "But then I've always liked teaching." She picked up her plate and carried it to the kitchen. Pouring detergent into the sink, she vowed that she would go out and ask Rick if he wanted her to go home, and if he wanted her to go, then she would. Absently she forced her right hand into a glass to wash it, then yelped in pain as the glass shattered in her hand. The cuts were not deep, but she would never be able to bandage them with her left hand. "Damn," she cried. "Rick, I need help!"

Rick was in the kitchen before she had finished the statement. Carefully he removed the broken remains of the glass from her hand as gently as he could, grasping her hand firmly when she flinched and tried to pull away. He held her fingers under the tap. Amy, disgusted with herself for the mishap, fumed silently as Rick sat her down on the daybed and rummaged around in the bathroom for the Band-Aid box. Amy obediently held up her injured hand so that Rick could apply the bandages. When he had finished she thanked him and smiled crookedly. "I was supposed to be helping you, and you end up having to help me again. Sorry."

Rick shrugged. "Is that why you came?" he asked. "To help me?"

"Yes," Amy said boldly. "Dr. Thompson said that you were in a bad way, and I thought maybe that you shouldn't be alone. You helped me more than once, remember?"

"I'm trying not to," Rick said bitterly.

Amy gasped with pain. "I'll leave, then," she choked. She jumped up and reached for her suitcase, but Rick caught her hand and sat her back down.

"I didn't mean that," he said hoarsely. "I'll take whatever time or anything else you can spare. Only don't go yet." Grief twisted his face and tears shimmered in his eyes.

"I know," Amy murmured soothingly. "I know you will miss Samantha. How is she?"

"It will be a long, hard road, but Samantha should eventually be all right. Meanwhile, the waiting's hell."

"I understand," Amy said soothingly. "You're missing the woman you love very much."

"You don't understand one damned thing!" Rick spat. "For somebody who's supposed to be so smart, you sure can be stupid!"

Indignation flared in Amy. Never in her twenty-seven years had anyone dared call her stupid. "I'd like to know what in the hell you mean, Rick Patterson, when you say that I'm stupid! Damn it, I came up here, against my better judgment, to try to help you because you miss the woman you love. And you start yelling that I'm stupid!"

"Well, you are," Rick snarled. "I've been missing the woman I love for the past three months, ever since she cut me out of her life in one knife stroke."

They both looked startled by the admission. Amy recovered first. "That's all well and good, but the things I said the night we quarreled still hold."

"Yes, I realize that you're probably right," Rick said. "I'd never fit in to that brainy world that you live in. Maybe we just weren't meant to be. I could never satisfy you."

"Oh, you could satisfy me all right, Rick," Amy returned sadly. "You could satisfy me in every way that mattered. Don't you understand? I could never satisfy you!"

Rick sat down in the big chair and lit a cigarette. "Amy, we need to talk. If we are ever going to get this mess settled, we have to start communicating somewhere else besides in bed."

Amy pulled up a dining chair and straddled it, leaning her forearms across the back. "All right," she challenged him softly. "Start communicating."

"Now, tell me," Rick demanded. "Exactly why do you think that you couldn't satisfy me?"

183

"Because Samantha couldn't," Amy replied firmly. She was trembling inside as she made the accusations, but she willed herself not to show it. Only the telltale twisting of her ring gave away her inner agitation. Rick looked bewildered, but Amy went on resolutely. "You were in love with her, and yet you were sleeping with Linda too, and then me. If Samantha, as lovely as she was, couldn't satisfy you, how on earth am I supposed to do it? I'm not the kind of woman who wants a casual relationship—"

"Excuse me," Rick said levelly. "Did I hear you say that I was sleeping with three women at once?"

Amy nodded. "I overheard you on the telephone the first day at Patterson's, making plans to christen Linda's waterbed. And then you and Samantha told me all about your trip to Mexico, and it was obvious that you hadn't been on the church choir tour. Now I know that you love Samantha—"

"Samantha and I went on that trip fifteen years ago, Amy," Rick said. "Our families have been friends ever since Samantha and I were kids. I worked for her while I was in college and she ran a small ad agency. Yes, we had an affair. I was not ashamed of it then and I'm not ashamed of it now," he added defiantly. "At the time I would have married her, but that wasn't what she wanted, and later I saw that she was right. I love her dearly, but now only as a mentor or a mother or a cherished friend. Would you believe me if I said that we haven't been lovers in years?"

Amy looked deep into Rick's eyes. "Yes. Yes, I would. And you rushed back to San Antonio because she had been hurt." Rick nodded faintly. "But that's just Samantha. Are you still going with Linda? Are you still sharing her waterbed?"

"It's a shame you didn't eavesdrop a little longer," Rick said dryly. "You would have heard me ask her how my younger brother and their new baby were doing. Linda is my sister-in-law, and she and my idiot little brother were having a party to celebrate the purchase of their new bed. That's all. Amy, I've never claimed to be a choirboy, but sleeping with three women is a bit much, even for me."

Amy took a deep breath. "I'm sorry," she said softly. "I'm glad I was wrong about your morals. But the problem is still there. I don't think I have what it takes to make you happy. You're warm, sensual, and passionate, and I'm not that way."

"Yes, you're all of those things," Rick argued quietly. "And more. You're a genius. Don't you realize that I spent that entire week up here agonizing over whether I could provide you with the intellectual companionship you need? And then when you told me to get lost, I decided that I couldn't, that you were right, so I didn't come back around to try and change your mind."

Amy sat and watched Rick light another cigarette. So he had been plagued by doubts, too. She had been so concerned with her own worries and fears that she failed to realize that he might have a few insecurities of his own. And they had been so wrong, both of them. "We're both a couple of insecure idiots," she said. Rick nodded. "I love you," she continued softly as Rick looked at her intently. "I know you're everything I want in a man. I'm sure, and I'll spend the rest of my life convincing you, if that's what it takes."

Rick smiled as he stubbed out his cigarette. "I love you, too," he said. "You satisfy me completely and always will, and I'll demonstrate that fact to you regularly for the rest of my life." He bounced out of the chair and reached for Amy. She pushed aside the dining room chair and reached for him, clinging wordlessly as tears of joy streamed from her eyes and wet Rick's shirt. He raised her face and kissed her with all the love and longing that he had stored up inside of him for the last three months. She met his passion with a flame of her own, the fires inside of her reaching out and engulfing Rick in their force.

Rick set her aside and reached for the daybed. He pushed it toward the other one as Amy ran into the kitchen and grabbed two strong lengths of rope. Rick positioned the beds together in the middle of the room, and with trembling fingers she lashed one set of legs together while Rick fumbled with the other ones. Amy found two pillows while Rick pulled off his shoes and shirt. He then pulled her to him and unceremoniously removed her clothes as quickly as he could. She reached down and unbuckled his belt, then tried to pull down his slacks and lost her balance, knocking him onto the bed. Rick grabbed her around the waist and jerked her on top of him, kicking his jeans and underwear across the floor as he rolled Amy onto her side and kissed her mouth and her throat. Shivers of pleasure coursed through Amy at the touch of Rick's mouth. She had thought that he would never touch her like this again, and she shook in his arms at the emotion that being with him again brought about in her. "Are you all right?" Rick asked as he felt her small body tremble."

"Oh, yes, I couldn't be any better!" Amy whispered against his throat.

He pulled away and looked into her face, and when he saw the love for him welling in her eyes, he understood her trembling, and his own body started to shake. "My, God, woman, you don't know how much I love you!"

"So show me," Amy whispered softly. "Show me, Rick."

As passion overtook them, they abandoned the frenzied haste with which they had come to bed. Slowly, sensuously, they explored each other's bodies again, touching and holding with flames of love no less real than the fire dancing in the fireplace. Only this time it was a new experience for both of them, because they knew that their actions were an expression of love for each other, and they accompanied their actions with whispered words of love.

"I just love to kiss you this way," Rick murmured as he took one small breast in his mouth and brought it to a hard peak of excitement.

"And I love to touch you like this," Amy murmured as she rubbed his stomach below his navel until he was moaning. Daringly Amy let her hand drift lower and caress his body intimately. The wind howled against the windows, but inside the cabin it was warm with emotion, and the sound of the crackling fire only added to their pleasure. She pushed Rick onto his back and pleasured him as he knew only she could, kissing and caressing his chest and stomach with her lips and her fingers, delighting in the tender quivering that her insistent mouth provoked. Rick lay back and let Amy touch him freely, tensing and moaning as she found his pleasure points again and tormented them with exquisite patience. He reached out with his long arms and rubbed her stomach and her waist with strong, tender fingers, causing Amy to throw her head back and moan in pleasure and anticipation. Oh, God, she thought, is this what it's like when you know you are loved? She knew by the expression on Rick's face that he was experiencing the same pleasure that she was feeling, and that thought drove her to greater daring. Reaching down, she caressed him with her fingers and her mouth, delighting in the sensations she was arousing in both Rick and herself.

Suddenly Rick grasped her waist and turned her over swiftly. "It's your turn," he whispered as he lovingly explored her body with his tongue. He nipped at her breasts with teasing lips, capturing one and tugging on it lightly until it became hard. Amy moaned softly and arched up to him, wanting to enjoy the feel of his mouth on her breast forever, yet knowing that there would be so much more in store for her in just a few moments. Rick slid his mouth down her stomach, caressing every inch of her warm flesh, while Amy squirmed beneath him with unconcealed longing. Finally his tongue drifted even lower, finding her sensitive femininity and tantalizing her until Amy thought she would explode. At last he possessed her completely, taking her in a wildness and a passion that made Amy lose her breath. Slowly they let the sensation build as they came to a loving crescendo, crying out together at fulfillment, and holding each other and sharing their warmth as the flames died to an ember. Rick brushed the hair away from Amy's forehead and kissed her there, then settled Amy beside him on the daybeds.

"I'm going to have to fatten you up," Rick teased as he stroked her body. "You've lost too much weight."

"I couldn't eat a lot of the time," she confessed. "I was upset and unhappy."

Rick reached out and planted a quick, hard kiss on her mouth. "That's over," he promised. "We'll fatten you up and make your tummy round." He stroked her flat stomach.

"You mean round like fat or round like pregnant?" she teased.

Rick's grin faded. He turned onto his back and put his hands under his head. "How would you feel about a child of yours if it wasn't brilliant?" he asked slowly.

Amy reached over and kissed him on the mouth. "Exactly the way you'd feel about one that was," she said gently. "It would be ours, and I'd love it." She got up and found a blanket, then returned to bed and pulled it over the two of them. "But who said anything about children? You haven't even proposed!"

"You already did that." Rick laughed. "So how does the end of January sound to you?"

"That's too long!" Amy protested.

"I know," Rick agreed. "But it will take us that long to get a wedding ready. We'll have to order invitations, buy you a dress, order flowers, line up attendants . . ."

"You want a big one?" Amy squealed in delight.

"Sure do, and so do you. Besides, how would it look if a wedding photographer eloped?"

Amy lay on the daybeds in front of the crackling fire and looked through Samantha's album. It was late, but she and Rick had slept for a lot of the afternoon, and now she felt relaxed and serene rather than sleepy. As Amy looked through the last pages Rick slid into bed beside her and put his arm around her shoulders. "You're going to miss her while she is in Houston," Amy murmured. Rick nodded wordlessly. "But it won't be forever. She can be godmother to our first child," Amy added.

"You're a generous woman," Rick said as he kissed her gently.

188

"I don't know about that," Amy said wryly as Rick looked at her in surprise. "I can't help but be a little jealous of her," she added honestly. At Rick's encouraging nod, she continued. "She's had so many years with you. Just look at all these pictures."

"Here's something that might make you feel better," Rick said. He handed her another album, admittedly thinner than Samantha's, but still substantial. She opened the album and caught her breath. In it was the picture that Rick had taken of her in the boat on Lake LBJ.

She turned the pages slowly. There were pictures of her in the office, in the studio, bent over the computer console, directing the attendants at a wedding, frowning over her microscope in the lab. There was one of her devouring a plate of food at a reception. There were some of the shots taken at Fort Wilson of Amy by the pool. She had not even realized that he had taken most of them.

"Go on," Rick murmured.

She turned the last pages. There she found the pictures that Rick had taken of her on the island. She gasped in amazement at her own beauty in the photographs. "You've made me beautiful!" she exclaimed. Her heart swelled with love and pride. She knew that she was seeing herself through Rick's eyes. That was how she looked to him. Suddenly she felt very humble.

"Those pictures are a portrait of my love," he said softly. "I recorded you the way that I see you." He leaned over and kissed her lightly on her forehead.

"What are you going to do with these?" she teased as she ran her finger down one of them. "Make a poster for the living room?"

"Sure, Patterson's is equipped to do that kind of thing." He laughed as he caught the horrified look on her face. "No, Amy, these are mine." His face took on a faraway look. "Seriously, I'm going to put them away, and when I'm a very old man I'm going to get them out and remember how lucky I was."

Amy was too moved to speak. Tears of joy shimmered in her eyes and wet her cheeks. She reached up and gently rubbed her lips against his chest.

"And that's not all," Rick said. "This is only the first album. I'm going to take your wedding portrait. I want pictures of you pregnant with our babies, holding our newborns, rolling in the grass with our children. I want you to pose with your new book and all the ones after it, and I want to do the pictures for those books to come. And I want to take your picture the day you become the department chairman."

Amy folded the album leaves together. "I dedicated my book to you," she said softly.

"Oh, Amy," Rick said as he kissed her tenderly. "I'm so honored." She reached out to him and held him fiercely, then Rick grinned suddenly. "That's a lot of posing I have planned for you," he said wickedly. "Are you up to it?"

"I wouldn't miss it for anything," Amy replied joyously. Rick set the album aside and reached for Amy, enveloping her in his warm embrace. Amy melted into him, reflecting as passion overtook her that this truly was a portrait of love.

LOOK FOR NEXT MONTH'S
CANDLELIGHT ECSTASY ROMANCES®

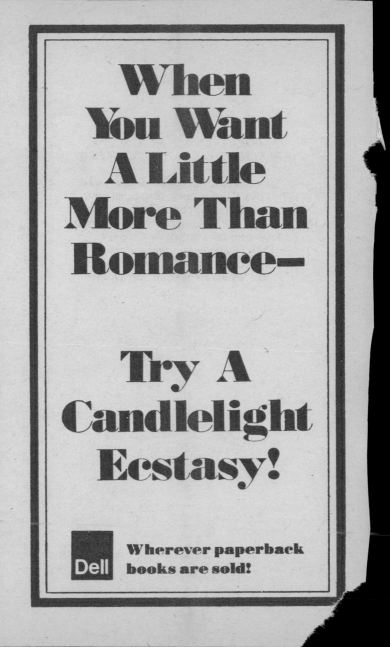